ACPL ITEM

P9-EDX-844

DISCARDED

"YOUNG ... me, and ... faces plastered all over every paper from here to Los Angeles,"

Dash exaggerated. "I'll expose every illegal thing you've ever even *thought* of doing—from jaywalking to littering."

"Oh, wow, I'm really scared." Billy let out his Woody Woodpecker laugh.

"You oughtta be. You're a sick bunch of losers," Dash lashed out. "The reason you hate so much is because you're so pathetic yourselves."

Billy's face turned red, then purple with rage. This time, the skinhead leader struck out with his fist. It connected solidly with Dash's left cheekbone.

Dash felt his head spin, and pain exploded in his face. Warm blood spurted from his nose and trickled down his chin. The gang closed in. This was it. He was about to be beaten so badly his parents wouldn't even recognize him.

Don't miss these books
in the exciting FRESHMAN DORM series

Freshman Dorm
Freshman Lies
Freshman Guys
Freshman Nights
Freshman Dreams
Freshman Games
Freshman Loves
Freshman Secrets
Freshman Schemes
Freshman Changes
Freshman Fling
Freshman Rivals
Freshman Heartbreak
Freshman Flames
Freshman Choices
Freshman Feud
Freshman Follies
Freshman Wedding
Freshman Promises
Freshman Summer
Freshman Affair
Freshman Truths
Freshman Scandal
Freshman Christmas
Freshman Roommate
Freshman Obsession

And, coming soon . . .

Freshman Taboo

ATTENTION: ORGANIZATIONS AND CORPORATIONS

Most HarperPaperbacks are available at special quantity discounts for bulk purchases for sales promotions, premiums, or fund-raising. For information, please call or write:
**Special Markets Department, HarperCollins Publishers,
10 East 53rd Street, New York, N.Y. 10022.
Telephone: (212) 207-7528. Fax: (212) 207-7222.**

FRESHMAN HEAT

LINDA A. COONEY

HarperPaperbacks

A Division of HarperCollinsPublishers

If you purchased this book without a cover, you should be aware that this book is stolen property. It was reported as "unsold and destroyed" to the publisher and neither the author nor the publisher has received any payment for this "stripped book."

This is a work of fiction. The characters, incidents, and dialogues are products of the author's imagination and are not to be construed as real. Any resemblance to actual events or persons, living or dead, is entirely coincidental.

HarperPaperbacks *A Division of* HarperCollins*Publishers*
10 East 53rd Street, New York, N.Y. 10022

Copyright © 1993 by Linda Alper and Kevin Cooney
All rights reserved. No part of this book may be used or reproduced in any manner whatsoever without written permission of the publisher, except in the case of brief quotations embodied in critical articles and reviews. For information address HarperCollins*Publishers*,
10 East 53rd Street, New York, N.Y. 10022.

Cover illustration by Tony Greco

First printing: March 1993

Printed in the United States of America

HarperPaperbacks and colophon are trademarks of HarperCollins*Publishers*

❖ 10 9 8 7 6 5 4 3 2 1

Thanks to Margot Becker R.

One

Dash Ramirez watched the steam rise from Lauren Turnbell-Smythe's coffee cup and mix with her slightly curly blond hair. For a moment, the University Café and everyone in it faded from Dash's mind—everyone but Lauren.

Dash daydreamed that it was like old times again. Lauren wasn't pissed off at him. Later on, they'd rendezvous back at one of their rooms to work on their new article for the *University of Springfield Weekly Journal*. Their intimate study breaks had always been a high point.

"Well?" Lauren's annoyed voice broke into Dash's daydream.

"Um, uh . . ." Dash stuttered.

Across the table, Lauren, who was wearing an oversize bowling shirt with the name Ralph embroidered over one pocket, and a long, black, thrift-store skirt which hid the five pounds she was always losing and gaining again, tried not to look at Dash. Next to her, Greg Sukamaki smiled knowingly. Greg was the editor-in-chief of the *Journal.*

"Wow," Greg commented wryly. He shook his head, and his straight, black bangs flopped in his face. "I'm used to newspaper staff spacing out when I yell at them, not when I'm offering to feature their next article on the front page of the *Journal.* Come on, Ramirez. Get with it."

Two sophomore girls at the next table looked over at Dash and giggled. They were splitting a basket of fries and ignoring a psychology textbook open on the table in front of them. Across the all-but-empty café, a boy with a tall, flat-topped afro and a redheaded girl were posting signs for U of S's UNITY Week—a multicultural celebration of the arts. Piles of fliers announcing campus events had been placed on the radiator in the front of the café. The smell of burning burgers wafted out of the kitchen.

Greg looked from Dash to Lauren and back. "Like I said, your last 'His and Hers' column on sexual harassment blew the whole campus away. And let's not forget your first co-authored article on fraternity hazing, which had all of Greek Row up in arms. I want another article just as provocative, just as insightful."

"I'm listening," Lauren said.

She looked accusingly at Dash. He knew he should be concentrating. But it was so hard when there was so much he'd left unsaid with Lauren. Sometimes Dash thought there were two Laurens—the soft, uncertain, innocent girl who'd come to U of S and the angry, bitter one who'd developed over the year. The one who cared about every hurt creature she met, and the person who'd fly off the handle at the littlest thing. The girl Dash had fallen in love with, and the one who'd spent the last couple of weeks telling him to blow off.

But then, maybe there weren't really two Laurens. She only raged when she saw some injustice in the world. Didn't that come from caring about everyone and everything so much? She'd been disappointed in society for not being sensitive to people in need and at Dash for not being sensitive to her. Her feminism had grown out of seeing how bad a lot of women had it. Dash really couldn't fault her for that.

Lauren picked up her cup and sloshed coffee onto the heavy wooden table. Flustered, she began mopping up the spill with a couple of paper napkins. Her slightly chubby cheeks were flushed. Dash knew this wasn't any easier on her than it was on him.

"You know, Dash, we can't get this column out if *I'm* doing all the work," Lauren said softly, balling up the napkins and putting them in the middle of the table.

A snide retort sprang to Dash's lips. In the nick of time, he swallowed it. If he ever wanted to get back together with Lauren, he had to be nice.

"Uh, I'm trying. Really," Dash said.

His brown eyes gazed into Lauren's violet ones. She bit a nail, then looked away. Dash felt miserable. They could hardly even hold a conversation. He stared down at the ink spots on his ripped T-shirt and poked with his toe at a loose nail coming up out of the sole of his heavy black motorcycle boots. Then he nervously adjusted the red bandanna he wore tied around his unkempt black hair.

"Look, you guys," Greg said. "If you're going to get all uptight with each other, do it on your own time. I called a meeting today because I need an article out of you." He banged his fist on the rough, graffiti-marred table. Coffee splashed onto it. "And I expect you to deliver."

Dash racked his brain, searching for a brilliant idea. Getting an article printed on the front page was a big honor. He wanted desperately to impress Greg—and Lauren. But all that came to mind were a few lame possibilities.

"Uh, I, uh, heard some freshman woman just debuted on a prime-time TV series." He knew it was a crummy idea for a story even as he was suggesting it.

Lauren shook her head definitively. "That's hardly front page news," she said. "Besides, there's no female/male spin on that story. It would make a lousy 'Hers and His' column." Ever since Lauren had begun exploring feminism, she'd started putting "Hers" first.

"So?" Dash said. "Maybe we should try something new—like doing a 'His and Hers' about something people don't think about when they think of gender."

Greg shrugged and smiled sympathetically at Dash. "Sorry, Ramirez. I've got to agree with Lauren on this one. Your last column worked because guys and girls have different takes on sexual harassment."

"*Women,*" Lauren protested under her breath. She drained her coffee cup, then motioned for the waiter to refill it.

Dash swallowed hard. Actually, he had his own ideas about why the last column had worked. There'd been a lot of tension between him and Lauren. Personal tension.

The sexual harassment complaint they'd covered had been brought by Courtney Conner, the president of Tri Beta sorority. It just so happened that Dash had ended a fling with Courtney at the time. A miserable and unhappy fling, but a fling nonetheless. Lauren had been jealous. And she'd been angry. And that had given the article a spark no reader could miss.

Dash resisted the urge to light up a cigarette. Lauren was always needling him about quitting smoking. A waiter pushed open the kitchen door and hurried over with a coffee pot to refill Lauren's cup. From out of the kitchen, a reggae rap tune on a radio poured out for a moment, then was cut off as the door swung shut.

Something about the music jogged an idea in Dash's mind. On the posters for UNITY Week, a black woman in African dress, an Indian man in a turban, and a Russian woman with a scarf tied over her head all smiled at Dash.

"Hey, I've got it!" Dash snapped his fingers. "How about writing something on UNITY Week?"

"Hmm," Greg said.

"Uh, I don't know about that," Lauren objected.

"No, really, let's think this out some more," Dash insisted, trying to be diplomatic.

He got up, sauntered over to one of the rainbow-colored posters, and examined the listing of events on it. The UNITY celebration would be kicked off that coming Saturday night with the One World Dance. There'd also be art shows, films, concerts, and workshops. Famous artists and writers from around the world had been invited to U of S to give special lectures. He and Lauren were sure to find something controversial to write about.

But as Dash ambled back to the table, he could see that Lauren was frowning. She was dead set against it.

Dash felt himself growing angry. He *knew* UNITY Week was just Lauren's kind of thing. She was really into multiculturalism. But just because *he'd* brought it up, she was treating it as though it were a free trip to Dante's *Inferno*.

Face it, Dash thought. *Lauren would nix any idea you thought up, even if it was guaranteed to win a Pulitzer.*

But Dash just sat down, picked up his cup, and took a swallow of coffee. He tried to think of something to say to break through the invisible wall that had sprung up between him and Lauren. "We could explore the race relations angle from the *positive* side," he said finally. "Most newspapers wait until something *negative* has happened before they'll print a word."

Lauren put her hands on the table and rested her chin on top of her hands, thinking. For a moment, Dash was sure he'd gotten to her. She was finally seeing it his way.

Then Lauren sat up and shook her head. "Look, there's a reason why no one writes about the positive stuff. People aren't interested. They want to see drama, fire!"

"I still think there's a story somewhere here," Dash insisted. "It'd be interesting to take a male/female view on something that wasn't so obvious."

"Sounds pointless," Lauren retorted. She stared into the dark swirls of her coffee cup.

Greg laughed and pushed back his chair. "Good, at least you two are talking. Keep at it till you come up with something hot. And make it soon, huh?" He stood up, took a last swig of coffee, and left.

Dash leaned back in his chair, studying Lauren's

unhappy face. Greg was right, he thought. It had been a long time since he and Lauren had really talked. In fact, Dash even felt kind of grateful to Greg for getting them to sit down at the same table together.

Lauren glanced up for a moment, and Dash tried a half smile. She looked away from him.

On the other hand, Dash thought, *working with Lauren could be a real picnic—complete with ants and rain clouds.* It was depressing that their relationship had sunk so low. He and Lauren had always really connected on feelings and ideas. Their relationship hadn't been purely physical, as his fling with Courtney had been.

The uncomfortable moment lengthened. From the kitchen came a clattering of dishes and the faint sound of the radio. The two sophomore girls were discussing possible questions for their next psychology quiz. A group of jocks were laughing loudly and devouring carbohydrates in a corner booth. The silence from Lauren was deafening.

"Look, Lauren . . ." Dash began, feeling a series of emotions sweep over him—anger, frustration, and deep, deep sadness. "I . . ." Suddenly Dash didn't know what to say. He grasped for words, anything that would break the suffocating silence. "I—wish this wasn't so hard."

Lauren moaned. "It's hard for me, too, Dash. And it will only get harder if we try and get personal. Our relationship is over. It's going to remain over."

Dash felt incredibly sad. He was sure that, deep down, Lauren still felt something for him. Something strong.

"I hoped—"

"For a while, I did, too," Lauren interrupted. "But it's unrealistic. For a while, I thought we could be friends, but even that hasn't worked out." She licked her lips and rubbed a hand across her face. "The last nice thing you did for me was tell me about that magazine internship. Let's leave it at that and just limit our relationship to the column from now on."

The internship. Dash had been so busy trying to break through to Lauren, he'd practically forgotten about it. Recently, he'd heard about a temporary stint at *West Coast Woman*, a magazine in Springfield. He'd decided not to apply for it himself, to keep from competing with Lauren. He'd hoped that would prove to her that he really cared. But like everything else he'd tried, it seemed to have failed.

"How *did* that intern application go?" Dash asked. With a fingertip Lauren traced some initials carved deep into the wood of the table. She still wouldn't look at Dash.

"I—sent in my application a week or so ago," she said softly. "They said they'd be making a decision in the next two weeks. I'm crossing my fingers and hoping." She lifted her face and stared right into Dash's eyes. Her eyes had lost a little of their unhappy glaze.

"I hope you get the job," Dash said simply.

"Thanks," she said. "I'm glad you told me about it."

Dash grinned. He could see the old Lauren now, peeking out from behind her new, cool, reserved facade. She wanted to make contact. She missed him, too.

"You deserve it," Dash said.

Lauren looked at him, as if to respond, then suddenly she was all business again. "Look, maybe we shouldn't go on with this chit-chat," she said tersely. "We've got a lot of work to do for 'Hers and His'—and I don't think the UNITY Week idea's going to get us anywhere."

Dash balled his hands into fists. Lauren could be completely infuriating with that closed-off, distant expression on her face. Her face. The one he used to spend hours kissing in the middle of the night after they and the rest of the newspaper staff had put the journal to bed.

Slowly Dash unclenched his fists. "Lauren, how about giving UNITY Week a break? I have a couple of friends over at the Latin American House who've been working on it. We could drive over there and talk to them, see if they can give us any tips."

A frown clouded Lauren's features. "I don't have my jeep with me," she said.

"But I have *El Toro*."

"Who's Eltora?"

"*El Toro*. The Bull. That's what I call my car."

Lauren looked up, her expression surprised and open for the first time all morning. "Your what?"

"I just bought a new car," Dash explained. "Actually, it's not new at all. It's a sixty-seven Chevy I got for a couple hundred bucks. It started running fine—or at least, it started running period—after I put in a few afternoons tinkering with the engine."

Lauren's expression was soft, friendly. "I'd love to Dash"—Dash could feel himself breaking into a grin—"but I just don't think it's a good idea," she finished.

Dash's stomach felt as if it had dropped to his toes. He shrugged and raised his hands as if to say, "I give up." Frustration overpowered him. "I tried, Lauren, I really tried," he said roughly. "All

I did was ask you to take a little spin in my totally hip, classic car. It's got to be way more fun than cruising in that big, white yuppie-mobile of yours."

His tone was sarcastic, harsh. For an instant, he saw hurt flash across Lauren's soft, delicate face. Out of the corner of his eye, he could see the psychology students at the table next to them listening and staring. He felt like a real jerk.

But in the next instant Lauren slammed him back.

"Hey—my car's completely gas-efficient. I bet your clunker burns up a whole tank getting to the gas station."

Dash leaned forward, his face close to Lauren's. She pulled back a little. "Yeah, but I've got lots of friends to ride in *El Toro* with me," Dash said angrily. "With your attitude, you'll be riding around in your Jeep all alone."

"Well, from the sound of it, fancy, uptight Courtney Conner's not going to set foot in *your* junk heap."

"What's that supposed to mean?" he growled. If Lauren was looking for a fight, she was going to get one.

"Just that you fooled most of the campus with your last 'Hers and His' column, but you haven't fooled me. You had a personal stake in it. It was a total whitewash job."

Lauren's words burned into Dash. "Are you accusing me of bad journalism?" he gasped.

"*Yes!*"

Dash snapped. "Now listen here," he said, pointing his finger into Lauren's face. "My relationship with Courtney had nothing to do with what I wrote about the sexual harassment case. I was just following my journalistic instincts."

"Great. You seem to be following a lot of instincts with Ms. Conner."

Dash felt a surge of anger. He grabbed Lauren's wrist and held it tight. They were so close, Dash could smell her herbal flower shampoo. Her cheeks flushed red, and her eyes sparkled with fury.

Dash caught his breath and bit off his next nasty response. Lauren *liked* arguing with him, he realized in a flash. She hadn't looked so alive and passionate all morning. And, he decided, he liked it, too. At least it was better than holding back every spontaneous thought or idea he had. For the first time all day, the real Dash Ramirez was talking to the real Lauren Turnbell-Smythe.

Lauren neatly twisted her wrist out of Dash's grasp. "That's what my course in women's self-defense taught me," she whispered. But Dash could see she was as excited at their closeness as he was.

"Neat trick," Dash murmured.

"I'm out of here," Lauren responded. She stood up and strode toward the door. "And your idea for our next column stinks," she added.

She grabbed something off the front radiator by the door, where students stacked piles of fliers announcing campus events. Lauren's face was red with rage. She crumpled up the flier and threw it as hard as she could at Dash. It landed in one of the coffee cups on the table. Then she turned toward the door.

"So, come up with a better idea," Dash shouted at her retreating figure.

"I will," Lauren yelled back.

As Dash watched the door swing shut behind Lauren, a strange smile played over his lips. Things weren't over between them, he was sure. Far from it. If they were, he wouldn't be able to push her buttons with a single comment. She wouldn't get so angry. She wouldn't care.

But, Dash was realizing, his old tactics of being sweet and nice weren't working. They didn't leave her any way to express her own anger at him, which was clearly boiling. When he fought, she could fight, too, and that made her feel good. Dash tapped his fingers against the table, thinking hard. Well, if Lauren wanted arguments, she was making it easy. Real easy.

Dash took the wet, crumpled paper Lauren had thrown out of the coffee cup and spread it on the table, smoothing out the wrinkles. He found himself staring at a flier for UNITY Week. There was a rainbow logo on the top, and a schedule of lectures, workshops, and performances with a listing of the countries where the speakers and artists were from—Morocco to Russia, Greece to Argentina. But that wasn't all that was written on the flier. In thick black marker, someone had drawn a swastika.

Dash's heart pounded out a staccato rhythm. The swastika stood for everything that was twisted and wrong in the world. The Nazis had killed six million Jewish people during World War II. Who could have brought their disgusting symbol to U of S?

Dash lurched to his feet, feeling sick, and stumbled over to the radiator. From among the piles of announcements, he grabbed the UNITY fliers. He flipped through them, hoping not to find any others that had been marked up.

Jews Suck! The disgusting words had been

scrawled across a flier in the same thick black marker. He looked at another one. *Kill all Niggers!* As he flipped through the pile, there were more words of hate and more swastikas. And there was another strange symbol Dash had never seen before. A snake with beady eyes and a knife clenched in its mouth.

It was a joke, some kind of violent, deformed joke, Dash thought. It had to be. Graffiti like this just didn't happen at U of S.

In a blinding rage, Dash ripped the defiled fliers into tiny pieces. He buried them at the bottom of the nearest trash can, then heaped some used napkins and paper plates on top. He felt dirty just from having read the words.

How did you deal with something so sick and horrifying? he wondered. You tried to forget.

Dash lit up a cigarette. He inhaled deeply then stalked out of the café.

Two

"Hey, pass the spackle!"

"What's spackle?"

"That goopy white stuff in the bucket, yo-yo."

"Well, how am I supposed to know? At home, we *hire* people to do this kind of work."

Schrkk, schrrkk, schhrrkk.

KC Angeletti listened to the scraping of her spatula against the Tri Beta house wall. The usually spotless living room was covered in dust, and the expensive couches had been moved into the middle of the room. The smell of plaster permeated the air. A dozen sorority sisters and pledges scraped along with KC. Next week, they'd don painters' caps and give the living room walls a new coat of pearl pink paint. It wasn't that the building was run-down, but when you were a Tri Beta, you wanted your house to be perfect.

The sorority president Courtney Conner walked down the row of slightly sweaty Tri Betas. None of the pledges had ever seen her so dressed down. She was wearing a pair of old shorts and a plain mint green T-shirt. But even in old clothes, Courtney looked perfect. With her aristocratic features, ash blond hair, clear brown eyes, and pale skin, she looked good in anything.

Schrkk, schrrkk, schhrrkk went KC's scraper.

Courtney stopped behind KC and gave her a friendly pat on the back. "Good work," she said.

KC smiled tightly. "Thanks."

Of course KC had more experience with wall scrapers and paint rollers than the rest of the Tri Betas. She hadn't been born with a silver spoon in her mouth. More like a pair of second-hand chopsticks. At her parents' health food restaurant, her family had done everything themselves, from cooking to serving to fixing broken chairs.

"Kimberly's due any minute," Courtney whispered to KC. "I'm kind of nervous. You'll back me up, right?"

"Uh, sure, Courtney. Of course I will."

A grim expression flitted across KC's delicate features, and the nostrils of her trim, aquiline nose flared. A long strand of her black hair had escaped from her French twist, and she flung it back with a toss of her head. Her long legs ached from standing so long.

The fact was, she didn't feel comfortable backing up her friend this time. Courtney had invited Kimberly Dayton to fill in the Tri Betas about UNITY Week. And while there was nothing wrong with bringing multicultural awareness to the campus, KC felt that Kimberly's visit wasn't going to go over well with the rest of the girls.

Bing, bong, bong, bing Tri Beta's doorbell chimed.

Courtney hurried to get the door. In a moment, she returned with a tall, slim black girl in a maroon dance skirt and a tank top made of African cloth. KC knew Kimberly because KC's best friend from high school, Faith Crowley, lived next door to her in Coleridge Hall. Kimberly's hair was swept up into a bun. Though she'd switched majors from dance to science, she still had the look—and the strong, lithe body—of a dancer.

KC smiled at Kimberly and waved as she walked in. The other girls looked up. Some of them seemed annoyed.

"Hey, everyone. This is Kimberly," Courtney announced. She wrapped her arm around Kimberly's shoulders and gave her a friendly squeeze.

"I invited Kim over," she continued, "to fill us in on UNITY Week. I know how excited we all are. So, take a break and sit down while she tells us about it."

With a sinking feeling in the pit of her stomach, KC watched Marcia Tabbert and Diane Woo exchange an annoyed glance. There were a few weak hellos.

KC tossed her scraper into the tool box and sat down cross-legged on the floor between Kelly Heald and Annie Neill.

"She invited a *stranger* over when we're all looking like *this?*" Marcia whispered in a horrified tone. She ran a hand through her chin-length, baby-fine auburn hair.

KC pressed her lips together. In a way, Marcia was right. Tri Beta had an image of impeccable beauty and untarnished class to uphold. Courtney shouldn't have asked Kimberly to come when they were about as put-together as Godzilla.

Courtney hadn't heard the comment, or else she had the class to ignore it.

KC looked around. Fortunately, a few of the

other Tri Betas seemed less put-off by Kimberly's visit. Kelly and Annie, for instance, seemed really interested.

Kimberly dropped her big shoulder bag on a sofa and sat down next to it. Courtney brushed off some of the dust on the other end and primly sat down.

"Hi, everyone," Kimberly began. "The UNITY events kick off the day after tomorrow, on Saturday, with an art show. Later that night, there's the One World Dance. We're going to be playing pop and rock music from all over the world. Should be a great chance to dance your feet off." Kimberly did a little shimmy with her shoulders and laughed.

Courtney giggled, too, and tried a shimmy of her own. KC saw Diane blush and throw Marcia another look. KC had to admit that Courtney was acting very un-Courtney-like.

"Then," Kimberly went on, "there's going to be a week of incredible lectures, performances, workshops, and special tutorials." She dug in her bag, pulled out fliers, and handed them around. KC noticed that a few of the girls scanned the listings curiously. But Marcia and Diane were still sulking, and that kept some of the others from showing their enthusiasm.

"The guest I'm really excited about is Rico Santoya," Kimberly gushed.

She pulled a book from her bag and held it up. It was called *Meditations in Black*. On the back cover was a picture of a light-skinned black man with piercing brown eyes, long, thick dreadlocks, and a scruffy little goatee. She flipped open the book and read a few lines:

> *"In school they teach you English.*
> *At work they pay you pennies.*
> *And still you dance on the lonely Spanish Harlem*
> *streets wrapped in the the colors of*
> *the Puerto Rican flag."*

Diane, Marcia, Lisa Jean, and Marina shrugged and looked at each other uncomfortably. They clearly didn't get the poem—or didn't care about it. KC wasn't quite sure she got it, either. She'd have to hear it again. But Annie was leaning forward, her eyes excited and intent. Kelly was smiling and nodding.

"Rico's mother is Caribbean, his father is half Puerto Rican and half Nicaraguan, and he was born in New York City, in the Bronx," Kimberly said. "He's incredible. Lyrical, street-smart . . . and he's never been to college himself!"

"I saw him on TV recently," Courtney informed her sisters. "I'm going to see if the university library has any of his books."

KC could see Marcia and Diane giggling into their hands. Actually, it *was* funny to imagine Courtney marching over to the library in her gold earrings and pearls and demanding a part in the New Harlem Renaissance. But rudeness was forbidden in the Tri Beta code—the girls shouldn't be laughing, KC thought. Feeling uncomfortable, she picked at a piece of plaster sticking to her sweatshirt. She wished Kimberly's visit were over and things could get back to normal.

But Kimberly wasn't through yet. "We'll also feature the Futures of Film Festival starting next Thursday and ending on Friday—twenty-four straight hours of movies and videos by emerging world artists. We'll wrap up UNITY on Saturday night with an outdoor jazz concert on the green. So come, bring a picnic, bring your friends."

KC knew for sure she'd be at the concert. Her boyfriend, campus deejay Cody Wainwright, was the emcee for the concert; he would be introducing the musicians. Her high school friends Faith and Winnie would be there with their crowds. There was no way she'd miss it.

"Well, I'm impressed," Courtney said, turning

to Kimberly. "UNITY must have taken weeks of planning."

"It did," Kimberly said.

"I feel bad. Tri Beta didn't lift a finger to help," Courtney went on. "Is there anything we can do to help now?"

"Actually," Kimberly said slowly, "there is. The posters for the event have been disappearing as soon as we put them up. I'm sure they're decorating rooms all over campus this very minute. But it does mean we have to keep going around and putting up new ones."

Courtney turned to the rest of her sorority sisters and gave them a big smile. "Volunteers? We could go out now for a couple of hours."

Annie and Kelly waved their hands in the air. Some of the other girls looked at one another unenthusiastically, shrugged, then slowly got up, wiping plaster dust off their rears.

KC got up, too. She stared for a moment at Marcia and Diane, who hadn't moved a muscle. She had no desire to go running around campus putting up someone else's posters. But Courtney was her friend and the sorority president. She'd asked KC to stick by her, and KC wasn't going to let her down.

"Hey, wait a minute," Marcia spoke up.

"Yes?" Courtney asked.

"We've got to finish prepping this place. We're supposed to paint it next week. The guys from Omega Delta Tau are all set to come help us on Thursday. We can't just blow them off." She motioned with one hand toward the walls, chipped with plaster.

For a moment, Courtney's face hardened. Then her expression changed. "You've got a point," she said. She motioned to some of the girls. "You stick around and work on the house with Marcia and the others. The rest of us will go with Kimberly." She waved her hand, herding KC and the other girls toward the door.

"Uh, Courtney," Kelly muttered.

"What?"

Kelly pointed to her plaster-flaked polo shirt with the ripped pocket.

A look of horror crept across Courtney's face. "Omigosh, we can't go out like this," she gasped. "Everyone, upstairs, wash up, and change. *Then* we'll put up posters."

"I'll wait outside," Kimberly said, picking up her bag and heading toward the door.

As the group went upstairs, Courtney talked about how great UNITY Week was going to be. KC started to follow her sisters upstairs, but a nasty giggle behind her halted her in her tracks.

"So, what do you think of UNITY 101?" Diane hissed to Marcia.

"Sounds fine. It's Courtney that's not quite right." Marcia giggled back. KC turned. She was shocked by the mean tone.

"No lie," Diane said.

"She's changed. Ever since her sexual harassment suit, she's become so—political." Marcia laughed. "I mean, I don't mind doing good deeds now and then, but she wants us to volunteer at the soup kitchen every single week."

KC watched the others drink up Marcia's disdain for Courtney. A few laughed nervously. She noticed that none of them had picked up their scrapers and gotten back to peeling the plaster.

"Hey, there's nothing wrong with being political," KC said. She stood by the foot of the stairs, her hands on her hips.

Diane shook her silky hair and leaned back against the wall, her long legs stretched in front of her. "No, there isn't. But Courtney's forcing it on the whole sorority."

A few of the other girls nodded their heads. "Uh-huh."

"It's true."

KC twisted a strand of her hair, feeling torn. In a way, the others were right. It was great that

Courtney had stood up for herself during the sexual harassment suit. But now she was trying to change Tri Beta as well. And the girls weren't ready for it.

"This *is* Beta Beta Beta, not the Progressive Students' Coalition," Marcia drawled.

"We've got traditions to uphold," Diane continued.

"We can hardly do that by hanging around with weirdo poets like that Richie Santarino." Marcia picked a little piece of chipped plaster out from under one of her perfectly filed nails and flicked it away.

"That's Rico Santoya," KC corrected.

"Whoever he is, he's not my idea of the perfect date." Diane giggled. The other girls giggled, too.

"Did you see that hair?" Diane messed up her own black, silky locks, set a tough, intense expression on her face, and held a paintbrush to her chin to imitate Rico's goatee.

Lisa Jean made a face. "Give me a nice, clean-shaven ODT guy any day of the week."

"I hope Courtney doesn't decide to go to the One World Dance with Rico as her escort," Marcia said.

Diane rolled her eyes. "After she brought that hoodlum Dash Ramirez to the Rosebud Dance with his boots and dirty T-shirt, anything's possible."

KC took a deep breath. It was true Courtney should never have brought Dash to the Rosebud

Dance. But the event clearly hadn't been any fun for Courtney, either. The other girls could have had a little compassion.

KC had had plenty of heartaches herself lately. Her father had lost a long, horrible battle with cancer. Then she'd found out she was adopted and gone through an emotional meeting with her birth mother. Things had never seemed so hopeless. And worrying about what the Tri Betas were saying behind her back had only made everything a whole lot harder.

KC scuffed the toe of her shoe against the polished wooden floor. "Listen," she said. "With this harassment suit, Courtney's been having a hard time. She needs our support, not nasty comments behind her back." She could feel the blood rushing to her face as her emotions heated up.

"Honestly, KC, we were only joking," Diane said.

Marcia nodded, her green eyes flashing. "The thing is, we've got to keep an eye on Courtney. I mean, if she keeps going with this embarrassing trend of hers, the whole sorority could go down."

"And that means you, too, KC," Diane reminded her.

KC's throat felt parched. She could feel a vein pulsing insistently in her temple. "Maybe you're right," she whispered. "But what good is a sorority anyway if every time something goes wrong, we just stab each other in the back!"

Marcia gasped. Diane blushed bright red. KC didn't stick around to hear what else they and the other Tri Betas had to say. She fled. Somewhere, far away, KC heard a door slamming. Then she realized it was she herself who'd slammed it. Her heart was pounding as she ran down the steps of the sorority house, past Kimberly who was sitting there, waiting.

What had she done? KC thought. She'd yelled at her sisters. She'd run out on Courtney and the poster squad. And the worst part of it was, she wasn't sure which side she was really on. Marcia and Diane were wrong, but so was Courtney.

Outside the air was cool and crisp, and a light breeze wafted clouds across the sky. Across the street a group of ODT guys were tossing a football on their lawn.

KC's cheeks burned. She'd been out of line. Yelling at the others was totally un-Tri-Beta behavior. KC knew she should walk back up the clean marble steps of the house and apologize, then join Courtney and the others to put up posters.

But she just couldn't face it. After taking a few deep breaths to try to calm herself, she started down the street. She was suddenly aware of how ridiculous she must look with her plaster covered sweatshirt and dusty face. She certainly wasn't doing her part to uphold the Tri Beta image. She should have washed up before she stormed out.

"What a beautiful woman," a guy with a southern accent drawled behind her.

KC spun around—right into Cody Wainwright's arms.

Cody's large gold-brown eyes stared at her lovingly. His dark brown hair was pulled into a ponytail, and a green canvas bookbag hung casually over one shoulder. He wore a fringed suede vest over a plaid flannel shirt. His long legs looked good in his faded blue jeans and beat-up cowboy boots.

"Oh," she gasped in relief. "I'm so glad to see you."

She leaned over and gave her boyfriend a kiss on the cheek. He quickly pulled her into an embrace, bringing his mouth to hers, kissing her passionately and holding her close. The moment lengthened.

KC smiled. She could feel the tension draining away. After her great love, Peter Dvorsky, had left for Italy, she'd thought she'd never meet anyone again. Frankly, she hadn't really wanted to.

But it had been so hard being alone when her father had died. Then she'd made an appearance on Cody's popular campus radio show. They'd had a big fight and she had stormed out. But later on, they'd gotten to know each other.

Cody had been so sweet. And just around that time she'd found out that Peter was seeing another woman in Europe. Being together with Cody just felt right. It was so comfortable.

KC linked arms with Cody, and they headed toward campus. A girl watering the Kappa Alpha Gamma lawn waved at them. "So what brings you over to frat/sorority row? Thinking of rushing ODT?" KC teased Cody.

Cody laughed. "Course not. I came to see you."

KC smiled. "That's sweet."

Cody stopped walking suddenly and pulled KC close. He let his bag slip to the ground. "I wanted to know if you'll be comin' to the UNITY dance with me on Saturday night," he said.

KC grinned. "Sure." She'd just assumed they'd be going together anyway.

They were standing at the entrance to the U of S Botanical Gardens, a gorgeous plot of land kept up by students in the botany department. The perfume of the different flowers scented the air. Red, orange, pink, and purple tulips rustled in the breeze. KC drank up the feeling of Cody's warm breath against her neck. His lips caressed her cheeks and her mouth. His arms held her tight. She caressed his back, feeling his long ponytail beneath her fingers. Then Cody stood back a little. Gently he took KC's chin in his hand and tilted her face up to his.

"Darlin', I . . . have a confession to make."

KC trailed a finger from the bridge of Cody's nose down to the tip. "Oooh, sounds serious," she said with a grin. "Tell, tell."

Cody's face was calm, happy. "KC Angeletti, I love you."

KC froze, her finger just curling over the tip of Cody's nose. Then her hand went limp and dropped down to her side. "Oh," she gasped.

"I realized it this mornin'," Cody explained casually. "I was cleanin' out the radio station, and I came across that tape of the first time you visited me on my program." He laughed. "Wow, did you give me a hard time."

KC froze. Cody kept talking, but KC's mind kept rolling over his first declaration. He loved her. Did she want his love? Maybe. But what about the commitment it involved?

"Our argument was totally different when I was listenin' to it on tape," Cody was saying. His southern accent was gentle and soothing. "It showed you're an honest person, KC. That day on the radio show you said what you thought. You know how important that is to me. And so I figured I better be just as honest with you, and tell you how I really feel."

KC pressed her lips together, too surprised to utter a sound. Her relationship with Cody had been so sweet, so casual. After all the pressure she'd been through, dating him had been different— she'd thought.

KC felt as though her mouth were stuffed with cotton. "Cody . . ." she croaked, not knowing what to say.

But her reaction didn't seem to faze him. "Shhh." He put his finger to her lips. "Don't say a word."

He held her close, cradling her head against his shoulder. She could smell the suede of his vest mixed with the clean, soapy scent of his shampoo.

"I know, you're scared. We weren't supposed to fall in love. Just be together. Just have fun." KC listened to the words pour out of Cody as if they were flowing out of her own mouth. "Peter was the big love in your life," he went on. "I'm just someone who's nice to hold and care about."

KC muttered a sound that was halfway between yes and no.

"It's okay," Cody's soft, warm, Tennessee drawl reassured her. "My love doesn't have any strings. It's a gift from me to you. I don't want anything from you in return."

"You don't?" KC asked.

Cody shook his head. "No. KC, we enjoy each

other. Let's keep doin' that, whether you're ready to say you love me, too, or not. All you need to do is keep on being honest."

KC stared at Cody, wide-eyed. "But—"

Cody cut her off. "KC, I mean it. No strings. No expectations. Just me, the same old Cody Wainwright you've always known, and you, honest, beautiful KC Angeletti." He gave her hand a little squeeze as if to reassure her everything was all right.

KC looked away. Cody said things didn't have to change, but KC knew they would. Right now, he said he didn't need her to say more. But later, he would. That was the way relationships were. Cody's arms around her waist no longer felt so reassuring and relaxing. They felt . . . demanding.

KC shrugged away from Cody's embrace. Things had been so comfortable. Why did they suddenly have to change?

Three

Melissa McDormand wandered up the row of art exhibits that lined McClaren Plaza. Sun poured down from the clear, bright sky. A breeze rustled the cherry trees. Melissa stretched her tight, muscular runner's body and shook her fiery red hair. Up and down the plaza, people strolled, talked, and looked at art set up in little square wooden stalls. Old, ivy-covered buildings surrounded the plaza. It was the perfect way to spend Saturday afternoon, unwinding after a week of classes and studying.

Melissa squinted at a stall displaying a series of photographs showing life in a black South African shantytown. The sad, desolate scenes seemed so out of place at U of S.

"Hey, Mel, look at this!"

Lauren, Melissa's roommate, had discovered a stall with bright, multicolored blouses from Central America. She was bent over a pile of them, her secondhand, thrift shop pants fitting snugly at the rear, and her paisley tie clashing with the weavings.

Melissa ambled over, her sneakers squeaking against the brick walkway. The Achilles tendon of her right leg let out a twinge of pain. Melissa stood still until it went away. During a recent Olympic trial race, she'd injured her leg and gone spilling onto the track in burning agony. Since then, her doctor had ordered her not to run, not to train, and not even to work out. She might never be able to run again.

Running was Melissa's life—or it had been up until now. She felt as if someone had snatched away her identity and left a blank, aching hole in its place. Thank goodness they hadn't taken away her U of S track suit and workout clothes, or she wouldn't have had anything to wear.

Melissa pulled her purple and gold official U of S track team sweatshirt around her. She looked through the colorful shirts, but her mind was somewhere else. She turned over price labels, barely seeing the numbers on them.

It was tough. She didn't really know what to do with herself now that she couldn't race. But she was trying to keep distracted—for instance, by taking in the UNITY Week art show when Lauren had invited her.

Her roommate threw her a warm but tentative smile. "Great stuff here, isn't there?"

Melissa nodded. "Yeah. Thanks for bringing me along."

Lauren grinned. "No problem."

Lauren looked longingly at one very intricately embroidered shirt. It was expensive, but then, Lauren could afford it. She was rich, unlike Melissa, who was at U of S on an athletic scholarship and had to make every penny count. That was another reason why the injury worried her so much. If she couldn't run, she just might have to leave U of S behind—along with her dream of becoming a doctor. Melissa sighed, trying to shrug off her worries. There was nothing she could do about them. She ambled on to the next stall.

Lauren paid for the shirt and hurried to catch up with her. Spending time with Lauren felt odd but nice. Recently, Melissa had had a falling-out with her roommate. In fact, she'd pretty much had a falling out with *everyone*. She'd been taking steroids to boost her racing performance, and they'd made her violent and out of control. She'd taken her hostility out on a lot of people. Now, she had a lot of patching up to do. Luckily, her friends didn't seem to be holding grudges.

There was a moment of silence between the girls as they walked. The shouts of people calling to friends or talking to artists intruded. Melissa felt awkward. She and Lauren were both trying, but things still weren't natural between them.

"So, what's up in your life?" Melissa asked.

At a stall of ornately carved drums with figures and faces on the side, a man was busily sculpting a large piece of wood. Melissa and Lauren stopped to watch.

Lauren sighed heavily. "The usual is what's up. I'm still waiting to find out if I'll get the internship at *West Coast Woman*. And looking for a subject for 'Hers and His.'" She wrinkled her nose and made a face. "Dash wants to write about UNITY Week, but I've got a tip I think will really turn this campus upside down—a possible scandal at the campus ROTC office."

"ROTC? You mean that army training course for college guys?"

"ROTC's for girls, too," Lauren said. "That's the scandal."

"What?"

"More sexual harassment—maybe." Lauren paused, letting the weight of her words sink in. "I've got to find out more. Dash's story would be boring. I *know* I can come up with something better."

Lauren's eyes sparkled. Her cheeks were flushed. Melissa wasn't sure if it was the newspaper scoop that excited her, or if it was the idea of beating out Dash. Poor Lauren. Maybe she never would get over him.

"I'm sure something really nasty is going on," Lauren chattered on. "I've just got to infiltrate and find out for sure. Brooks said—" Suddenly she cut herself off in mid-sentence. Gasping, she clasped her hand over her mouth.

Melissa swallowed hard. "Is that who gave you the tip? Brooks?"

Lauren nodded, looking numb.

Melissa closed her eyes for a moment, then opened them. The campus was still there, students still haggled with artists over the prices of their work. The world hadn't fallen apart and disintegrated just because someone had mentioned her ex-fiancé.

"Lauren, it's okay," Melissa said. "I'm over Brooks now."

Lauren bit her lip. "Yeah, I know." But she didn't sound too certain.

After all, Melissa thought, *just a little while ago, I was beating Brooks Baldwin over the head in a steroid frenzy. If I were Lauren, I probably wouldn't believe me, either.*

For a long time, Melissa had thought she'd never get over the shame and embarrassment of being left standing in her wedding dress at the altar. For months and months afterward, she had felt devastated.

But after she'd tried to deck Brooks at Winnie Gottlieb's party, she realized things were out of hand. As she'd watched her life slowly evaporating, she realized that her depressed feelings were more about being dumped than about not sharing the rest of her life with Brooks. That relationship had never really been meant to last.

Now, Melissa was going on with her life, apart from Brooks. The sound of his name no longer stung her the way it had a few months ago. Hearing his name made her feel only a very dull throb.

"Look," Lauren tried again. "I'm really sorry."

"It doesn't matter," Melissa said with a wave of her hand. "I ran into Brooks at the student union the other day. He told me he joined ROTC." It wasn't true. She made her voice sound light and airy to reassure Lauren.

But Lauren wasn't buying it. "I didn't mean—"

Melissa cut her off. "Forget it," she said. "Really."

Silence descended. The mood of tentative friendship between them was broken. Awkwardly, Lauren turned and suddenly got very interested in the sculptor and his drums. Melissa sighed. It was going to take longer than one afternoon to win back the trust and easy comfort of her friends.

"Hey, Lauren, Mel," came a shout from across the plaza.

Melissa squinted into the sun. Liza Ruff was screaming at them from the shade of the ivy-covered buildings. Liza's red hair looked practically electric in the sunlight, and it clashed horribly with her tight, orange sweater and plaid leggings. Next to her, Faith Crowley fidgeted, looking a little embarrassed at Liza's outburst. Faith's long blond hair was pulled back in a high ponytail, and her flouncy peasant skirt brushed the tops of her cowboy boots. Beside them, Kimberly surveyed the crowd along the plaza, as if she could make everything go perfectly at this first UNITY Week event just by willing it. Melissa hurried over with Lauren, glad that something had come up to break the tension.

"Hiya," Liza said.

"Hi," Melissa said.

"How's the movie star business going?" Lauren asked Liza.

"TV, darling, TV," Liza replied, gesturing wildly with her hands.

Liza had recently won a small part in a television pilot, and she'd been impossible ever since. Well, actually, Liza had been impossible before that. It was just stronger now.

Faith grinned. "I'm trying to convince Liza to come back once she's a big star and do a part in one of my shows. You know, get the publicity happening."

"Well, of course I will, Faith," Liza gushed. "Roommates have to stick together—even after one of them is living in a mansion off Rodeo Drive."

Kimberly glanced down at her oversize red and yellow watch. "Listen," she cut in. "We're supposed to meet Winnie, Josh, and Clifford for the Tanya Jacobson lecture. She's going to be talking about what it's like to be the first woman of color to be chosen for the Museum of Modern Art's retrospective. Why don't you come?"

"Why not? Sounds great," Lauren said.

Melissa pursed her mouth. As interesting as the

lecture sounded, she just wasn't ready to face all her old friends together. The last time she had was at Winnie's party, when she'd beaned Brooks. She had plenty of bridges to build before she could just throw herself into the social scene again.

"Uh, I think I've had enough art for one day," Melissa said, not looking her friends in the face. "My Achilles tendon could probably use a rest, too."

"You sure?" Lauren asked. There was a guilty look in her eyes, as if Melissa's decision was somehow her fault. Melissa threw her a smile and nodded.

As the others hurried off, a bittersweet feeling came over Melissa. Trying to shake it off, he stopped at a stall featuring abstract paintings by a young Native American artist. The painter, who'd dyed half of his jet black hair bright purple, was arguing passionately with an aesthetics teacher about color theory. Melissa listened for a while, then moved on. A tall, heavyset girl was handing out fliers listing future UNITY events. Behind her, a bank of UNITY posters lined one of the red brick walls. A few were torn, and someone had taped them back together with yellow masking tape. Melissa walked slowly down the brick path, feeling alone in the crowd.

Suddenly she stopped in her tracks. A blond guy

in a green headband was slowly making his way through the crowd in a wheelchair. His powerful upper body flexed beneath his tight, sleeveless purple T-shirt. He wore dirty, tan, fingerless gloves that protected his hands as he wheeled. His thin legs were hidden beneath a pair of baggy sweatpants. A few sketch pads and pencils protruded from the big knapsack that was slung over the back of the chair.

Danny Markham was part of the reason Melissa had been able to get up and face the world after her tumble at the Olympic trials and her flirtation with steroids. She'd met him at the gym. She hadn't even realized he was paralyzed until he'd wheeled out from behind the weight machine.

Danny was a real inspiration. Once, he'd been a baseball player, a total jock, just like Melissa. Then there'd been the accident. His spinal cord had been severed. Danny would never walk again. Compared to facing life in a wheelchair, she had decided that being stood up at the altar and her other problems were about as serious as blowing soap bubbles.

And then there'd been that kiss.

At first, it had stunned Melissa. Danny had seemed a little stunned, too. But at that moment, she felt something she'd missed ever since Brooks got cold feet. Physical comfort. Connection. And intense attraction.

Melissa had been thinking about that kiss for almost a week. There was something right about the two of them together. Danny was the first guy who'd ever come right out and said he thought she was angry at the whole darn world. And he hadn't been scared off by it, because he was just as angry himself. Part of Melissa wasn't sure she could really get close to a guy in a wheelchair. But another part of her wanted to find out more. She'd come by his dorm room and left a few messages. Up until now, though, there'd been no sign of him.

Melissa watched Danny navigate through the plaza, packed with people. Everyone seemed to be ignoring him.

"Excuse me, but your briefcase is in my face," Danny wisecracked to a professor whose rear end was directly between him and an exhibit of Chinese ink-drawn cartoons. The teacher turned bright red when she saw Danny's chair, and she moved quickly out of the way. She turned her back, and Danny made a face at her. Melissa cracked up.

Danny wheeled over and stared intently at the drawings. He was a cartoonist himself. He was probably busy stealing material at this very moment, Melissa thought.

She marched up to him. "Danny!" she said.

Danny lifted one gloved hand in a casual wave. "Melissa. Hi."

Melissa didn't believe his nonchalant air, not for a second. "Hi, yourself. Where've you been?" she demanded.

Danny shrugged. "Oh, just busy, I guess. You know how fascinating and action-packed life is for us paraplegics." He turned back to the cartoons, blocking Melissa out.

Melissa refused to be put off by his sarcasm. "Cut the crap, Markham. You've been avoiding me."

Danny hesitated a split second. Then he looked directly into Melissa's eyes, his expression innocent and open. "Now why would I be doing that?" he countered. But the moment's hesitation told Melissa she'd been on the mark.

"I don't know, Danny, why don't you tell me?"

Danny pursed his lips, tapping his fingers along the polished steel of his wheelchair. "Come on, Melissa. Don't make a big deal out of nothing. I was just busy."

Melissa opened her hands and shrugged. But inside, she was seething. How dare Danny kiss her and then pretend it was nothing. It *was* something, and they both knew it.

"Well, I was busy, too," Melissa lied. Actually, she was so lost without track, she'd been looking for ways to fill up her time. "But I took the trouble to come visit you anyway."

"Well, if you're so eager to see me, maybe you should ask me out on a date."

He sounded angry, Melissa thought. Or maybe he was just scared. It was hard to tell.

"Isn't that how these things usually get done?" he challenged when she didn't respond.

"Hard to do when you're avoiding my calls." Melissa crossed her arms over her chest, waiting for Danny's next crack. Danny Markham was not getting rid of her so easily, just because he sat in that wheelchair.

"Okay, well let's just make a date now, then. That is, if you don't mind dating a cripple." Danny's voice had a loud, hard, edge. The girl in the cartoon stall turned to stare, along with a few of the people admiring her work.

"Okay. No problem," Melissa said.

Danny's mouth dropped open, and he looked stunned.

Melissa stared at him, challenging him. "That's right, Danny, I'd like to see you." The people surrounding the cartoon stall were all listening now. "So how about it?" Melissa pushed.

She still wasn't totally sure how she felt about dating him. Well, actually, Danny himself was terrific. It was the wheelchair part that was sort of scary. But she could hardly back out now.

Suddenly the words began bursting out of Danny's mouth like bullets. "Okay, fine by me. You want to give it a go, I'll give it a go. How about wheeling me over to the One World Dance Saturday night? Maybe I'll get lucky, and your leg injury will flare up. Then I can sweep you off in my wheelchair for the fast numbers."

Danny's tone was sarcastic, as if he was sure Melissa would say no. But there was something else beneath it. A quaver in his voice. Danny meant the invitation, Melissa realized.

"The dance sounds great. Thanks for asking me," Melissa said simply.

"You're kidding! You'll go?"

"Sure, why not?"

Melissa was a little surprised to find that she meant those words completely. So what if she ended up hanging around the sidelines at the dance? She'd never been all that excited about jumping around with a bunch of sweaty college students anyway. Besides, it beat chasing Danny all over campus.

"All—all right. Then . . . I guess I'll see you at the gym, okay? Saturday night? Ten o'clock? Don't be late."

"I'll be there."

"Hope you don't mind heavy metal," Danny said. He patted the arm of his chair.

Melissa shook her head. "I wouldn't have said yes if I did." She threw Danny a grin. Then she waved, turned, and started down the brick path.

Danny's tenor voice boomed after her. "Don't expect me to be Michael Jackson on the dance floor. If my foot gets stuck on the pedal, I just ride around in little circles."

Melissa just laughed. "See you there," she called over her shoulder.

Four

· ·

Pound, pound, pound, pound, POUND.

The sound of Kimberly's hammer echoed through the empty gym. She stood up, brushed the dust off the knees of her jeans, and admired her handiwork. The gigantic world map tacked to the plywood board would make the perfect backdrop for that evening's One World Dance.

"Clifford, get the ladder!" Kimberly called.

"At your service," Clifford Bronton called back.

He grabbed the ladder and carried it across the gym floor. Bits of rainbow-colored confetti peppered his short, flat-topped afro and clung to his brown corduroy pants and tan, short-sleeved, button-down shirt. They'd spent over an hour tearing crepe paper into tiny pieces. Clifford's glasses sat slightly crooked on his nose.

The hinges of the ladder let out a loud squeak as Clifford set it up beneath the basketball backboard. He lifted up the map to hang it. "Josh, Winnie, and I can do this," Clifford said. He waved Kimberly away. "Go take care of more important stuff."

Winnie Gottlieb had half-climbed up one of the purple and gold gymnastics mats hanging from the gym wall. Her short, spiky hair stood out at all angles. Her oversize neon-green sweatshirt clashed with her big, plaid, boy's boxer shorts. Donald Duck earrings swung wildly from her earlobes. Josh Gaffey, Winnie's husband, was pulling on her arm, trying to get her to come down.

Winnie jumped to the ground, her white plastic go-go boots clacking against the shiny wooden floor. She patted her slightly bloated stomach. Her pregnancy wasn't quite showing yet.

"You OK in there, little girl?" Winnie said.

"Winnie," Josh said. "We don't know if it's a girl. It's an *it*."

Josh shook his head, and his shaggy brown hair flopped wildly. His small blue marble earring flashed on his earlobe. He wore a green T-shirt with a bleach stain, jeans with holes in the knees, and a pair of beat-up old sneakers with computer programming notes scribbled all over them. He played unthinkingly with the little woven bracelet around his left wrist. He messed Winnie's hair. She turned around and stuck out her tongue.

It was hard to imagine those two becoming parents, Clifford thought. Aloud he said, "Win, your baby isn't due for another six and a half months. This dance is happening tonight. Can I get some help before this map falls on my head?"

Rolling her eyes, Winnie walked over. "Well, you don't have to get all huffy about it."

As she buried her nose in her boxes of supplies, Kimberly tuned out her friends' friendly bickering. Tons of stuff still needed to be done. Luckily, Meredith Paxton, a theater tech whiz, and Robert Geary, an engineering student, had hooked up the two massive speakers that morning.

The big job would be twisting and hanging dozens of rolls of rainbow-colored crepe paper streamers. She had to tape up the posters of great thinkers, writers, activists, and artists from around the world and set up the refreshment tables. Courtney had promised to come by later with a bunch of her sorority sisters and help fill up ten dozen balloons with helium.

Putting on a dance was a lot of work, Kimberly thought. Maybe later, when the work was done, she'd have a chance to relax and get excited about it. But for now, staging a major campus event just seemed exhausting.

Well, the first thing to do was obviously to bring in the rest of the boxes of streamers from her van and start twisting. Earlier, they'd only unloaded about half the supplies.

"Hey, guys. You done with the map, yet?" Kimberly called across the gym.

"Just about," Clifford answered.

"Well, come help me out." Kimberly pushed open the safety bar of the gym's back exit and walked into the corridor. Earlier, she'd lined the walls with bright UNITY posters to announce upcoming events. Her friends followed, their shoes squeaking on the linoleum floor. They hurried out back to the parking lot where Kimberly had parked her beat-up old van.

"Yuck!" Kimberly exclaimed as she stepped over a rotten banana peel, a half-eaten peanut butter sandwich, and a pair of torn, smelly gym socks. Papers and other garbage lay strewn around the parking lot. Two trash cans lay upside down in the center of the pavement.

"What a mess," Josh said, staring in dismay at the chaos. "It wasn't like this when we came in earlier."

"Probably raccoons," Clifford decided.

"Ugh, the smell." Winnie held her stomach. "I think I'm getting morning sickness again."

"Win, it's the afternoon," Josh said.

"It's okay, I get it any time," she answered.

Kimberly tiptoed around the garbage and sped over to the open side-door of her vehicle. "Hey, Win, I thought I told you to lock up the van," she said, peering inside.

"Don't yell at me, I'm sick," Winnie begged. "Someday, you'll get pregnant yourself and you'll see."

But Kimberly wasn't listening. She was looking inside the van. The decorations for the One World Dance had been destroyed.

"Oh, no!" Kimberly moaned.

She held up posters of Indira Gandhi and Golda Meir, both completely shredded. Crepe paper lay unrolled and crumpled. Grape juice had been thrown all over the floor of the van.

Kimberly let the posters fall out of her fingers. She sat down on the pavement and buried her face in her hands. "Those were half the decorations for the gym," she cried.

The very words made her feel desperate. She and a dozen other students had spent weeks planning and working to make UNITY Week and the One World Dance a reality. Now, some creep had destroyed their opening party. Kimberly got up and pulled the soggy, torn decorations out of the van.

"Who would do something so mean?" Kimberly asked.

Clifford stepped over and slowly massaged Kimberly's tense shoulders. "Kim, calm down."

"It's downright vicious," she cried.

"Don't take it so personally," Clifford went on soothingly. His fingers made little circles on Kimberly's neck muscles. "I'm sure no one meant to ruin the dance. It was just vandalism. It happens everywhere—even on our safe U of S campus."

"That's right," Josh agreed. "It was probably some rowdy townies."

"Or drunk frat brats," Winnie chimed in.

Clifford'd fingers worked their magic, and Kimberly's anger began to subside. Her friends were right. There was no great conspiracy, just a gang of bored, stupid kids. But that still left the problem of the gym decorations.

"What are we going to do?" She groaned. "We've invited the entire campus to this dance, and when they show up, the gym is going to look ridiculous."

"I don't think so," Clifford countered. "You've still got half the decorations. I'll go downtown to Woolworth's and see what I can get there."

Kimberly paused, thinking. It would mean a lot more work and not much time to do it in, but she had her friends' help. Courtney's sorority sisters could pitch in when they showed up later, too. Clifford was right. They could pull it off.

Suddenly Kimberly was in her action mode. "Okay! Clifford, you take my van and hit Woolworth's." She fished in her pocket and tossed him the keys. "Josh, Winnie, you get back in that gym and start twisting crepe paper. I'll clean up here and join you in a minute." They didn't have a moment to waste.

"Yes, sir—I mean, ma'am," Winnie said and saluted. She grabbed Josh's hand and dragged him inside.

Clifford threw Kimberly a friendly wink. Then he jumped in the van and roared off. Kimberly bent down and righted the two overturned trash cans. Feeling like a woman with a mission, she began filling them with the ruined decorations.

"Looks like messy work," a soft voice said from behind.

Kimberly turned, a squashed can of bicycle oil in her hand. A light-skinned black guy in a T-shirt and sweatpants was staring at her, his hands on his hips, his head tilted cockily to one side. His wide brown eyes bored into Kimberly's face with a mixture of curiosity and amusement. He had classic features that could have gotten him onto the cover of any men's magazine. He'd obviously been out for a jog, there was a flush across his high cheekbones, and his short, black, wavy hair looked damp with perspiration.

Kimberly quickly dropped the greasy can into the trash, suddenly embarrassed.

The guy laughed, still staring at her. "So, what brings you out for clean-up duty? Is this your campus job?" There was a snide, almost mocking tone in his voice.

Kimberly shook her head, surprised at how unnerved she felt by his gaze. "No. I'm doing the decorations for the One World Dance tonight. There was some vandalism and well . . ." She waved a greasy hand as if she could make it all go away.

"The One World Dance? What's that?" the guy asked.

Kimberly frowned and stared at him. "What planet are you from? We've had signs up all over campus for the dance. It's the kickoff party for UNITY Week, and it's happening in this gym tonight, starting at nine."

The guy shrugged. Kimberly couldn't help staring at his slim, muscular chest. "Guess I missed the posters," he said.

Kimberly nodded. "I guess so. People have been stealing them as soon as we put them up. But haven't you heard *anything* about UNITY Week?" she asked.

The guy grinned. "Oh, sure. You've got a great bunch of artists pouring in here for the festival. Just goes to show you what a little pull a prestigious college name and a lot of money will do." It was a snobby comment but probably all too true, Kimberly decided.

She arched her back, stretching—all too aware that his eyes followed her curves as she moved. She felt both excited and embarrassed. "Well, I know *I'm* psyched about UNITY. I've been dying to meet some of these people for ages. Like, Anna Talltree, the Cree Indian dancer from the New York City Ballet, is going to teach some guest classes. And Rico Santoya's flying in from New York City, too. Have you ever read his poems?"

"I am acquainted with the man's work."

"His writing is great, isn't it?" Kimberly said enthusiastically.

"Brilliant," the guy agreed.

There was a hitch in his voice, and Kimberly

looked at him curiously. His charming, intelligent eyes caught hers and held them. There was a hint of a smile on his face.

"Hey, don't I know you from the Ujamaa Society?" she said, naming the black students' union on campus.

The guy shook his head. "I don't think so."

Kimberly snapped her fingers. "I know. Track team."

"Wrong again."

"Well, I'm sure I know you from somewhere."

The guy pursed his lips. "I don't think so. I don't even go to school here."

Kimberly felt stupid. Now, she could see that the guy was a little older than the average college student. No wonder he acted so cocky and self-assured.

"You don't?"

"Nope. Fact is, I don't believe in college. It's just some ivory tower where nothing *real* ever happens. Give me the music of the street, the color of human passion, the movement of the stars against the black night."

Kimberly stared at him, speechless. Whoever this guy was, he was a knock-out.

Kimberly recovered her poise quickly. "Well, um, some of us think you can find those things at U of S, too. If you're into music, we'll have the best at this dance tonight."

"You will, huh?"

"Yes," Kimberly said. "Why don't you show up and see for yourself?" She looked at him, trying to come off as flirtatious and sure of herself as he was.

The guy stared at Kimberly until she could feel herself blushing. "Will *you* be there?" he demanded.

Kimberly nodded.

"Then yeah, sure, I'll come," he said.

Kimberly grinned in spite of herself. "Great! It will be a blast."

He let out a belly laugh. "So, how about telling me your name?"

"I'm Kimberly. Kimberly Dayton."

"Okay, Kimberly Dayton, so I'll see you at your dance—just to check if you college kids really do know how to pick good music." He smiled and threw Kimberly a sexy wink. Then he turned and began jogging off.

"Hey, what's your name?" Kimberly called after the fast-retreating form.

The guy just let out another belly laugh and kept running. Kimberly watched his slender, attractive form disappear around the corner of the building. She wasn't quite sure, but she thought she'd just gotten a backhanded invitation to her own dance.

Five

....

"*L*eft face!"

Senior ROTC cadet Buck Sandler was screaming commands at a corp of freshman trainees in neatly ironed and pleated air force uniforms. The rows of cadets executed swift pivots on their heels, as if in one move. Buck glared at them, his crew cut wet with sweat. Brooks Baldwin turned along with the other trainees.

"What a way to spend a Saturday afternoon," Dash muttered, half to himself.

He'd wanted to hit the UNITY art show on McLaren Plaza, but Lauren had insisted that they come here. Sitting in Lauren's Jeep across the street from the training field, they could see everything without being observed themselves. Dash puffed away on a cigarette, following Brooks and the other trainees with his eyes.

"When are you going to quit smoking for good?" Lauren asked.

Dash swallowed a retort. Then he remembered the fire in Lauren's eyes last time when they'd argued. If the two of them were going to have any kind of relationship at all, it was going to be an honest one. If she bugged him, and he felt like bugging her back, he would.

Dash blew smoke in Lauren's face. "I'll quit smoking when I'm good and ready." Lauren turned her face away from the smoke and wrinkled her nose.

"About face!" yelled Buck, and the cadets obeyed.

The ROTC training grounds were in a rundown section of Springfield. Broken picket fences separated tiny plots of land with dilapidated houses on them. A few had old, rusted cars in the driveways.

"Ten hut!"

"This ROTC office sure is in a crummy neighborhood," Dash said, more to needle Lauren than anything else. "Maybe they're trying to toughen up their cadets by making them deal with street punks every time they come for training."

"At ease!"

"Very funny." Lauren sniffed. "But there *is* serious business going on here."

"Uh, Lauren, how about letting me in on exactly what we're going to expose them for?"

"Sexual harassment," Lauren said. She pointed her finger out the Jeep window straight at Buck Sandler, who was in the middle of another bulldog bark.

For a moment Dash was shocked. Then he put on a calm front. "I see."

Lauren pointed to a sweet-faced, earnest, cherry-blond cadet, one of the few women in the corps. The cadet spun into her left and right turns with quick, eager motions.

"That's Sarah Hunter," she continued. "Brooks heard Buck talking to her behind the shooting range, pressuring her for sex. If he's doing it to her, he could be doing it to other female recruits."

Dash closed his eyes and pressed two fingers against the bridge of his nose. He could feel a headache coming on. The whole sexual harassment episode with Courtney had been incredibly painful—not only for Courtney but for everyone who knew her. He took a long drag on his cigarette.

"Lauren," he said softly, "maybe this isn't the best idea."

Instantly Lauren's guard went up. She crossed her arms over her chest and glared. "Why not?"

"Well, we just did an article about harassment. Maybe we should try something else."

Lauren shook her head. "That doesn't help Sarah Hunter, does it?"

Dash jerked open the Jeep's ashtray compartment and ground out his cigarette. "Look, I know sexual harassment happens all the time. But I don't want to write about it over and over again."

Lauren snapped the ashtray compartment shut. "Why not?"

Dash sighed, wishing she'd just relax and try to see it his way. "These things are difficult," he said. "During Courtney's case, you took the man's side at first, while I was helping Courtney. If there's a cut-and-dried men's and women's point of view, how do you explain that?"

Lauren shook her head. "You're just jealous because I got a great scoop. *This* is the story to do." She pointed out the window at Buck.

Dash leaned his arm against the Jeep door and rested his head against the palm of one hand. He turned his back on the ROTC field, wishing he could drown out Buck Sandler's commands as easily.

"Fine. But there are *two* of us writing the column. Don't I get a say in what topic we choose?"

"Well, come up with a better idea," Lauren challenged.

"I've got a few of them," Dash said curtly.

"Like what?"

"Like one of the dance troupes coming here for UNITY week got its start in the Watts ghetto of L.A. And there's a painter from Peru seeking permanent asylum in the U.S."

Lauren rolled her eyes. "Fine, great, wonderful— if we weren't writing a column that's specifically about women's ideas versus guys'. We need a story with a strong female/male contrast, and that's exactly the story I've got."

Dash rubbed the back of his neck with one hand, trying to release some of the tension that seemed to build up every time he got within fifty feet of Lauren. Buck's screaming wasn't helping his headache any, either.

"Aww, Lauren, why do we have to write about something that's totally sexist? For a change, can't we write about our male/female views on music, poetry, food, or anything else in the world that's important to people—men and women?"

Then Lauren did something that stunned Dash. She laughed.

"Oh, Dash, you're such a kidder," Lauren said. She waved her hand, dismissing the idea completely.

"Lauren, I mean it."

Lauren giggled. "Incredible. I come up with an amazing scoop, and you're so jealous you just can't handle it. Come on, Dash. Keep an open mind."

"I am!" Dash yelled.

"Bull!" Lauren yelled back.

"Look, I can't work like this," Dash told her. "I'll just go away and come back when you've grown a new brain." He pushed open the Jeep door, got out, and slammed the door shut furiously.

"Good riddance," Lauren yelled after him.

Dash walked down down the street. His head pounded. His fingers twitched. Lauren was not making working together easy. Dash's long legs ate up the pavement, putting space between the two of them. He'd loved Lauren once. He still loved her. But sometimes, he just couldn't stand her.

It was too upsetting. Dash needed a cigarette. He pulled a crumpled pack out of his pocket. There were only a few tobacco crumbs and a book of damp matches in it. Dash vaguely remembered a twenty-four-hour convenience store around there somewhere.

Behind him, the ROTC cadets were shouting a marching chant. Down the block in front of him, Dash heard other shouting. He squinted against the sun. A group of people had gathered in front of the convenience store's dirty, torn awning. It looked like some kind of shoving match.

"Nick or Zow, Nick or Zow!"

The nonsense words drifted toward Dash. He could see six or seven guys standing in a circle, bending over something. A few of them were wearing flannel shirts and leather jackets. Others had on camouflage jackets and army boots. A few of the guys had shaved heads. Either that, Dash thought, or they had serious cases of premature baldness.

As Dash got closer, a chill ran up his spine. He'd suddenly realized what the group was shouting.

"Niggers out! Niggers out!"

They'd completely surrounded a black man who was kneeling on the ground, his hands over his ears. Dash's heart leapfrogged as he recognized Abraham Allen, a junior who was in one of his writing classes. Rage and fear twisted across Abraham's face. The white guys were screaming at him and shaking their fists in his face.

"Oh, no!" Dash gasped. He took off across the pavement, his engineer's boots clomping on the concrete. "Hey you!" Dash screamed as he ran.

The members of the group turned as he raced toward them. They assumed a military stance and waited. Behind them, Dash saw Abraham stagger to his feet and scoot out of the circle he'd been trapped in. He looked scared but unhurt. His baldheaded attackers forgot him as they focused on Dash.

Skinheads! Dash realized with disgust. He'd heard rumors that a branch of the racist, semimilitary group had sprung up around Springfield. He'd never believed the stories. He just hadn't been able to accept that anyone in this quiet, beautiful town could espouse the kind of ugly, ignorant, violent ideas the skinheads stood for.

Dash skidded to a stop in front of the waiting group. His hands were balled into fists, and he could feel the adrenaline pumping through his body. He was totally outnumbered. He knew he had to calm down, or he'd get creamed. He took three deep breaths before he opened his mouth.

"What exactly is going on here?" Dash asked. He kept his voice flat and unemotional.

The main skinhead cocked his head to one side and crossed his arms across his U.S. Marine flak jacket. He was a skinny, runty little guy, bald except for a little stubble. His blue eyes squinted suspiciously at Dash.

"I'll tell you what's going on here," the leader said. "My group is exercising our right to free speech, under the laws of the United States of America!"

Dash felt sick. As a journalist, he was all for free speech. But it didn't include terrorizing people. He noticed a tattoo that ran along one of the skinhead's neck. A snake with a dagger in its mouth. The same symbol Dash had seen scrawled with the anti-black and anti-Jewish slogans on the UNITY fliers.

"And your group is . . . ?"

The group of skinheads jumped to attention. "Youth for a Pure America!" they shouted in one voice. They threw out a straight-armed, heel-clicking Hitler salute.

"And I'm Billy Jones," the leader said, "head of the Springfield branch."

Dash's eyes bulged. The Springfield branch! Then that meant there were other neo-Nazi creeps like these running around the state. And probably other states as well.

Billy Jones leaned forward, staring into Dash's face. "Why are you so interested in us?" he demanded. "Go mind your own business. We're only protecting our rights!"

"*Your* rights? How's that?" Dash demanded.

The skinhead hitched up his pants and puffed out his chest. "These foreigners come in here and take all the jobs. Then there's nothing left for us Americans."

"Foreigner!" Abraham called out from the side. "I was born in a suburb outside of Denver."

"Shut up!" Billy screamed.

"You shut up!" Dash exploded.

The skinhead's blue eyes bored into Dash like a dentist's drill. "What's that accent I hear? You some kind of sicko foreigner, too?"

Dash fumed. When he was really upset, his faint Latino accent got stronger. What a time for it to kick in.

"Yeah, Billy," one of the other skinheads called. "I think this nigger lover's some kind of spick!"

The words stung Dash like acid. Back home in his upper-middle-class neighborhood, no one had ever used a racial slur against him or any of the black kids in the area—at least not to their faces.

Breathe, Dash told himself. *There are half a dozen of them. You can't take them all on, not even with Abraham's help.*

"Spick!" Billy Jones spat in Dash's face.

"Spick, spick," the other skinheads began screaming.

Dash turned his back. He walked over to

Abraham, put his arm around him, and started down the street. His heart was pounding. Part of him wanted to run back and see how Billy Jones looked with a fist down his throat. The smarter part just wanted to get out of there before he and Abraham got involuntary plastic surgery—without anesthesia.

The shouts trailed them down the block. Then Dash and Abraham turned the corner and broke into a run, heading as fast as they could toward the safety of campus.

A dozen blocks later, they stopped. Dash sank, gasping, onto the lawn in front of the student union. His throat burned from running. His head was spinning with fury and disbelief. All around him, students calmly went about their business, hanging out, reading, or chatting with their friends. Two guys were handing UNITY fliers to each student who walked by. Dash wanted to scream out, to tell everyone that something was very, very wrong in Springfield.

Abraham sank down next to him. "Thank heaven you came along. I thought they were going to kill me," he said.

"I've never seen anything like that before," Dash said. He forced his ragged breathing to slow down.

"We had some like them back home," Abraham said. "They beat up a friend of mine—put him in the hospital. Those skinheads aren't kidding."

"So, what do we do about it?" Dash asked. "Call the cops? Press charges?"

Abraham pulled at a blade of grass. He didn't say anything for a long time. Then he sighed. "Listen, the skinheads didn't push me. They didn't hurt me. What are the cops going to do?"

"Scare them out of doing it again?" Dash suggested.

Abraham shook his head. He stared out over the campus, a weary expression on his face. "Dash, that store's a block from my house. If those skinheads find out I'm the one who filed a complaint against them, they'll know exactly where to find me. And next time they catch me, I'm dead meat."

Dash leaned back, watching the busy, happy students passing by as he considered Abraham's words. His friend had a point. But if Abraham didn't speak out, the skinheads would just get away with it. And they'd keep on doing it. The scary thing was, Dash didn't get the feeling anyone at U of S really knew about these guys. He certainly hadn't believed in them until he'd run into them himself.

Abraham stood up and brushed some bits of grass off his pants. "Got to get going," he told Dash. He reached over, shook Dash's hand, then slapped him on the shoulder. "Thanks for helping me out. I owe you one." He got up to go.

"Just remember that next time you're critiquing one of my pieces in writing class!" Dash called after him. Abraham threw him an thumbs-up sign, and Dash laughed.

But inside he felt sick. The skinheads were a menace. They had to be stopped. The U of S student body had to be made aware of the evil lurking in Springfield. And as a *Journal* writer, he was in the perfect position to get the word out. If Lauren would agree to write about it, too.

Lauren. He wished he could talk to her right now, tell her every horrible word that Billy Jones and his gang had said. He knew she'd have a plan, some way to use their column to decimate the Youth for a Pure America.

Dash reached into his pocket, craving a cigarette, but he'd lost even the crinkled, empty pack. He leaned back in the cool, soft grass. It felt soothing, as though one thing, at least, was right in the world.

Six

. . . .

"**H**ello. Welcome to the One World Dance."

Kimberly had to talk loudly over the salsa beat pouring from the speaker. She took the bills the Indian girl and her blond boyfriend handed her. The couple linked arms and danced into the crowd.

The gym was a sea of gyrating colors—people in African Kente cloth, Chinese jackets, and Western clothes. Some had really dressed up for the event while others had decided to come casual. The gym walls looked bare, even with the rainbow streamers and balloons, but no one seemed to care.

"Hello. Come on in and enjoy One World," Kimberly said to the next person in line. She took a quick glance behind her at the dancers. A slow Spanish song was playing now. In the middle of the dance floor, Liza was camping it up with Clifford, pretending to swoon to the romantic Spanish lyrics, then breaking into a jig. Not too far away, Winnie and Josh held each other close, their hips moving to the beat. Winnie was wearing a silver lamé top and a matching floor-length skirt. Josh had thrown a tuxedo jacket over his usual jeans and T-shirt.

Kimberly greeted the next person in line. "Hi. Thanks for coming to One World."

"Kimberly. I see you got a promotion."

Kimberly stopped, her hand in the cash box. "Huh?"

"From sweeping up the trash this afternoon, I mean."

Piercing brown eyes stared into Kimberly's. The high cheekbones and model-perfect features wore a faint, sensual scowl. A black turtleneck and tight black jeans revealed a perfect, slim body.

Kimberly grinned. "Hey, Mr. Tall, Dark, and Mysterious."

She'd been wondering when the gorgeous guy from the parking lot would show. *If* he'd show.

She'd been kicking herself all night for not getting his name. And his number.

"That's me." He brought his face close to hers.

"So, what's your name?" Kimberly asked.

"On a night when the muses wail like electric guitars, names are not important, Kimberly. If the night sky invited you to dance, would you stop for introductions?"

Kimberly laughed. Everything about this guy was completely bewitching.

He grinned. "Now, how about it?"

"How about what?"

"Dancing!" He grabbed Kimberly's hand and spun her out of her seat behind the table. Her calf-length blue satin trumpet skirt whirled out around her.

"Wait a second! I've got to sell tickets!" Kimberly protested.

"Hey, who's in charge of tickets?" someone called from the back of the line of students waiting to get in.

But the guy with the piercing eyes already had one hand around Kimberly's waist, the other gently cupping her neck. He led her into the rhythm of the song, and she found her feet dancing in spite of themselves.

"Go ahead, Kim, I'll handle this," one of the

other dance organizers said. She began making change.

Kimberly's new dance partner twirled her off into the crowd before she could even say thanks. Instantly, she felt lost in the song, in the sweaty press of bodies, and in the gentle play of this stranger's hands against her back.

The One World Dance looked as though it was getting better and better . . .

KC nestled against Cody as they moved in rhythm to the lulling Latin drum. The beat echoed through the gym, drowning out the chattering students. She had on the sensational black dress Lauren had bought her at the beginning of the year. She knew she looked fabulous in it.

But for once, looking beautiful was actually making her feel uncomfortable. Would Cody love her more if she looked as if she'd just walked off the cover of *Glamour* magazine? Maybe she didn't want him to. Should she have toned down her outfit, just in case?

But another part of KC felt wonderful being beautiful. And especially wonderful knowing Cody noticed it.

"Happy?" Cody asked.

KC snuggled closer as they danced. "Completely." She hesitated a moment. Then she added, "But you know that doesn't mean—"

"I know," Cody said. "No commitment. Just my love and your good feelings."

It was funny. Three simple words, "I love you," and KC was feeling totally weird. But she knew she could trust Cody. Couldn't she? She tried to ignore the conflicting thoughts spinning in her mind.

KC wrapped her arms around Cody, swaying to the music and trying to stay relaxed. He'd traded in his flannel shirt for a Western shirt with fancy stitching. He wore a strand of turquoise beads around his neck. He was wearing his "good" cowboy boots, too, the ones without the rundown heels.

KC waved to Melissa and Lauren, who were standing in a corner by themselves. Lauren was pointing at someone over by the refreshment stand—Dash, KC realized. Melissa was glancing at her watch.

The song came to an end, and an up-tempo Arabic pop song poured out of the speakers. Cody threw KC an inviting smile and kept on moving to the beat. KC sighed. She just didn't feel like fast dancing.

"I'm sorry, Cody, I need to take a break."

Cody leaned over and kissed her, remaining totally mellow. "No problem, darlin'. Let's find some chairs, then get something to eat and drink."

He slipped his arm around her, and they made their way slowly through the crowd.

Cody's arm felt warm and soothing, KC thought. But should she be enjoying it? Was it fair when he loved her so much and she had Peter on her mind?

Peter Dvorsky. She'd loved him. She'd thought that love would last even when he won a photography award and hopped off to Florence, Italy, to a prestigious school. But now that was over. Peter had another girlfriend. And she was stuck with her old feelings. And Cody's new ones.

Cody found two empty chairs and sat KC down. "Save our seats," he shouted over the music. "I'll be back with some food in two shakes of a rattlesnake's tail."

KC watched him slip through the crowd. He stopped to say hello to Dash and Brooks, who stood by the refreshment table near the door. They were drinking frothy pink punch, eating pretzels and dip, and seemed to be arguing passionately. Cody began filling a paper plate.

In a few minutes, he was back, a few choice

treats arranged on the rainbow-colored plate. He handed it to her and turning the chair next to her backward, threw one lanky leg over it and sat down. He rested his hands on the back of the chair, and his chin on top of his hands.

"I picked out the best foods for you, darlin'." Cody nodded at KC's plate.

Cody was so nice. She wasn't being fair by not loving him more. She dug into her food, trying not to feel guilty.

"Hey!" Courtney popped her face in front of KC's. A few of the other Tri Beta sisters trailed along behind her.

Courtney was dressed in a stunning pink chiffon dress, with a string of pearls looped around her neck. Her ash blond hair was swept into a sophisticated chignon. A few of the other sisters were rocking subtly to the music. Marcia and Diane, sulking in the back, didn't.

"Great dance, isn't it?" Courtney said. She bopped a little awkwardly to the haunting Arabic melody.

"Uh-huh," KC murmured.

"You can bet on it," Cody agreed enthusiastically. "Great music, great food."

"Weird music," Diane muttered behind her.

Courtney pretended not to hear. "I'm just so

glad we could help. You know, Kimberly had some decorations vandalized. We spent the whole afternoon blowing up balloons and twisting crepe paper."

Diane and Marcia exchanged a glance and rolled their eyes. They looked as though they'd rather be eating rocks.

"Oh, hey, there's Paul Schultz and a couple of the ODT guys," Marcia said, pointing across the gym.

A few boys in sports jackets and slacks were standing near the huge map of the world. They were scanning through the crowd trying to pick out people they knew. The Tri Beta girls perked up when they saw they'd been spotted.

"Ooh, Matt Brunengo's with them." Regina Taylor giggled.

"Let's go say hi," suggested Cameron Abbott.

This time, it was Courtney who rolled her eyes. "Bye, KC. Bye, Cody. Duty calls." She swept across the gym in a whirl of pink chiffon, the others trailing behind her.

Cody laughed. "It looks like your sorority president and her sisters are not quite on the same wavelength," he commented. He reached out and took a piece of almond-honey cake off her plate.

"You can say that again," KC agreed.

"Which side are you on?" he asked. A few crumbs fell into his lap, and he brushed them off.

KC shrugged. She broke off a piece of halvah and ate it listlessly. "Well . . . half of me feels one way, and half of me feels another."

It seemed to be like that in other ways in her life right now, too. Especially with guys, she thought. Here she was with Cody, and she knew she really should be enjoying herself totally. But her mind was on Peter, who was off in Florence, probably devouring mounds of pasta with his new girlfriend at this very moment.

KC scanned the gym: Kimberly was in her partner's arms, Faith was joking with Meredith, and Dash and Brooks were still at the refreshment stand table, seemingly eating everything in sight. They all looked happy and content. Why couldn't she be, too? Because of Peter.

A guy with dark hair and round, yellow-framed glasses was handing money to the girl at the ticket desk. KC laughed at herself. Boy, she had Peter so much on the brain, people around her were even beginning to look like him. The guy strolling casually into the gym wasn't Peter though. Peter didn't wear fancy European jeans and yellow-framed glasses. He wore sloppy old clothes and wire-rimmed glasses.

KC watched as the guy waved to someone near the refreshment table. He broke into a big smile— the same warm, wide smile that confronted KC every time she looked at her old pictures of Peter.

"Omigosh," KC gasped.

The Peter lookalike was being greeted by Dash and Brooks. Only he wasn't a lookalike. He *was* Peter. Peter Dvorsky, back from Italy.

"Darlin', what is it?" Cody asked, concerned.

KC just stared numbly. Brooks extended his hand, and he and Peter shook. Dash gave Peter a hug and slapped him on the back. They were all grinning and talking a mile a minute. Soon, Winnie and Josh spotted Peter and came running over with hugs and greetings. Why was Peter here? KC wondered.

Dash began looking around the gym, waving his hand toward the dance floor. Peter scrutinized the crowd. They were looking for her, KC just knew it!

A flood of emotions overwhelmed her. Part of her wanted to run over and throw her arms around her old boyfriend. The other part was furious. Why had he left her in the first place? How could he have been so cold and remote when her father had been dying? Who was this Italian girl he'd replaced her with? And why, why, why had he come back to Springfield?

"KC, please, tell me what's wrong," Cody urged. His tone was gentle, but KC could hear urgency beneath it. He took her hand and squeezed it.

KC gulped back a sob. Cody loved her. Peter had left her. The choice should have been easy.

But it wasn't.

Confusion brewed in KC's brain. If she ran over to Peter, she would lose Cody's love—the only love she could count on right now. But if she walked over and slapped Peter's face, would that mean she'd made some kind of commitment to Cody—one she wasn't sure she was ready for?

All at once, KC just felt herself crack. She couldn't see Peter, and she couldn't not see him. She couldn't love Cody, and she couldn't not love him. But one thing she did know. She couldn't deal with it. Not here. Not now. Not in front of all these people.

"Cody, I . . . don't feel good. I don't feel very good at all." She held her stomach as if it ached. Well, at least she wasn't lying about that—she did feel pretty nauseated.

"Don't you worry. I'll get you home faster than a trout in a swift river." Cody took the plate out of KC's hand and dumped it into a nearby trash can. He helped her out of her chair. Then, his arm around her, Cody started toward the gym's front door.

"No!" KC gasped. If they went out the front, they'd pass right by Peter and the others.

Cody gave KC a confused look.

"I mean, uh, let's go out the back exit," KC told him. "It . . . it's closer to my dorm."

Cody still looked puzzled, but he said, "Okay." He turned, still holding onto KC, and pushed through the crowd. As KC put more and more bodies between her and Peter, her panic subsided. Cody pushed open the safety bar to the gym's back door, and the couple walked down the corridor. In a few minutes, they were outside, striding across the parking lot and toward Langston House, KC's dormitory.

The night air felt fresh and cool. KC breathed a sigh of relief. She'd escaped . . . at least for now.

"Peter Dvorsky!" Winnie exclaimed. She spun out of Josh's arms and hurried over to greet him.

Dash grinned. "Isn't it wild?"

Brooks nodded. "Showed up from Italy out of the blue."

Peter swept Winnie into a hug. His hair curled over one eye. He pushed his yellow-framed glasses onto his nose. It felt great to be back on campus. Italy had been an adventure. He'd made tremendous strides with his photography at the American College in Florence. But it was hard being away from home, too. He'd missed his friends.

"New style, Dvorsky?" Winnie pointed to Peter's Italian jeans, white linen button-down shirt, and yellow glasses.

Peter laughed. "I did kind of get Europeanized."

Josh slapped him on the back. "What brings you to our humble U of S dance?"

"Actually, I'm on my way home," Peter explained. "It's my parents' twenty-fifth wedding anniversary, and they flew me back for the party. I figured I might as well stop in and say hi." He made his voice sound casual, as though that was all there was to it. But it wasn't. One name pounded in his head. KC Angeletti. KC. KC. KC.

It had been months since they'd had a real conversation. He thought KC probably had figured out he'd been seeing someone else in Florence. It was time to clear the air—and get back to the love and companionship that had disappeared from his life when he left Springfield.

Even though Italy was great, and he had a girlfriend, Peter was lonely. His new girlfriend, Ursula, was fun, wild, and exciting, but they didn't talk much. They didn't share deep feelings and ideas the way he and KC had.

"How long will you be around?" Josh asked.

"This time, just for tonight. I'm off to my parents' tomorrow, but I'll be back later in the week for a few days. My return flight to Italy takes off a week from Monday."

"Oh, great," Winnie said. "Then you'll be around for the big outdoor jazz concert."

"When's that?" Peter asked.

"Next Saturday night," Winnie said. "It's the final event of UNITY week."

"Everyone will be there," Brooks added.

Peter drank the last of his soda. Everyone. KC, too. They'd fall in love all over again. He could see it.

Peter looked around the gym again, searching every corner. No KC anywhere. He didn't want to be obvious about seeking out KC, so he turned to Josh.

"So . . . what's new with you two?" Peter asked Winnie and Josh.

Josh grinned. "Well, we got married."

"No joke?"

"Uh-uh. And . . . we're pregnant!" Josh laughed happily.

Peter's eyes bulged, and he stared, amazed, at

Winnie's stomach. She immediately pulled up her silver lamé top and exposed her slightly rounded tummy.

"Here she is, little Sinead-Latifah. That's what I'm going to call the baby when she's born—after the Irish singer and the rap star," Winnie confided.

"Winnie!" Josh groaned.

Peter was silent for a moment, thinking. While he'd been off in Italy, people like Winnie and Josh had gone on with their relationships, made strides, taken steps. He'd just let things drop with KC. He felt suddenly as though time had left him behind. He had to see KC. He had to start catching back up. Right now.

"Uh . . . " Peter started. "Where . . . where's . . . "

"KC?" Winnie finished.

"Uh, yeah."

Winnie hummed to herself as she scanned the gym. "Hmm, can't see her anywhere now."

Dash motioned with his hands. "I saw her earlier over there with—" He cut himself off. "Um, with a bunch of her sorority sisters," he finished.

Peter smiled. "That figures. Those Tri Betas really stick together."

"Maybe she'll be around tomorrow," Josh said.

Peter tore at the paper cup he was still holding, his mind lost in images of KC. "No good," he said. "I'm out of here at eight-thirty in morning."

"But you'll be back later in the week?" Dash asked.

"Uh, yeah," Peter said absentmindedly.

He wasn't really listening. He'd flown thousands of miles to see KC. He didn't want to wait until next week. He'd just have to go find her at her dorm.

"Uh, listen guys, I'm kind of jet-lagged," Peter said. He tossed the remains of his paper cup into the garbage. "I think I'd better get some sleep."

Winnie pouted. "Come on, Dvorsky. Don't be a party pooper. Me and Sinead-Latifah want to dance with you."

Peter couldn't help laughing. A couple of dances couldn't hurt, he thought. After all, he'd missed his friends almost as much as he'd missed KC.

"Okay," Peter said.

Winnie grinned. "All right!"

She pulled Peter onto the dance floor. Josh, Dash, and Brooks stood on the side, watching and swaying slightly to the beat. Peter let the good feelings wash over him. It was great being home.

Seven

·······················

A rock and roll tune blasted out of the speakers and ricocheted off the gym walls as Melissa stood on the sidelines, scouring the crowd for a blond guy in a wheelchair. Lauren was standing beside her, trying to make herself heard over the music.

"So then Dash just got out of the car, slammed the door, and left," Lauren shouted. She was wearing the Guatemalan shirt she'd bought at the art sale that afternoon and a skirt made entirely of secondhand ties sewn together.

Melissa only half listened. When she'd accepted Danny's invitation to the dance, she hadn't thought about how hard it would be to spot a wheelchair in a crowd of dancing people.

"Dash was so rude," Lauren said, sounding hurt.

Melissa glanced at the clock behind the basketball backboard. The clock's blinking digital numbers said 10:20.

"But I'll show him," Lauren insisted. "When I get inside this ROTC scandal, I'll blow off Dash. Then I'll win the internship at *West Coast Woman* magazine and *really* wow him."

Melissa nervously swished the flared hem of her red cotton tank dress. She hadn't had anything special to wear, so Lauren had lent her an outfit. It fit her athletic body like a glove. She knew she looked great. But it reminded her of the last time she'd gotten dressed up: the day of her not-wedding.

"Give me your love. Give me your heart," crooned the singer. Melissa checked the clock again. 10:23.

"I can't believe I was ever so crazy about Dash," Lauren was saying incredulously.

Melissa felt anxious and alone. Lauren, who'd been so supportive earlier in the day, seemed to have forgotten all about Melissa's date. Seeing Dash seemed to have erased any other thoughts for her.

Poor Lauren. Melissa knew how awful it was to feel angry about a guy. She'd been the same about

Brooks. But now that was over. She was ready to open her heart to someone new. Now if only Danny would show up and give her a chance.

The blinking clock said 10:28.

Melissa felt a painful, panicky little feeling stirring deep inside her. She tried to soothe herself: something had held Danny up; he'd be there soon; he'd show.

"Guys. They can be so difficult," Lauren insisted.

The clock flipped to 10:30.

Face it, Melissa told herself. *He isn't coming.*

She felt sick, betrayed. Why had he done this to her? Didn't he care how terrible she'd feel? Melissa tried to control her feelings. *No big deal*, she tried to convince herself. *It's all very simple. Danny Markham stood you up!*

But the fact was, it hurt. It hadn't been easy opening herself up to someone new. For a long time, she'd wallowed in the pain of being alone and unloved without Brooks. It had taken courage to let herself like Danny.

Lauren was still ranting about Dash. For an instant, Melissa felt just the same way. It wasn't fair.

But then she sighed and let the angry feeling go. She'd wasted too much time being furious at Brooks. She'd put her track career, her friendships—her entire life—on the line.

Little by little, she'd come to realize that the world didn't owe her anything. Neither did Danny. If he'd liked her the way she liked him, he would have shown up. He hadn't. It was a pretty clear statement on his part.

"You can't count on a guy," Lauren went on. "You've just got to be strong and stand on your own two feet."

Melissa smiled wearily and tried to tune into what her roommate was saying. She looked out over the dancing, happy crowd, trying not to feel so desperately alone.

Kimberly's partner spun her into a triple turn. He caught her and held her close as the final chords of the song faded. Kimberly could feel his solid, muscular body against hers.

They'd been dancing half the night without a moment's break. Kimberly hadn't asked his name again. He, on the other hand, kept whispering hers all night long.

Kimberly was impressed. Salsa, Afro-pop, or American rock, this guy could dance to them all. During the slow songs, he held her close and whispered bits of poetry, his breath hot against her ears.

A samba was the next tune, and Kimberly's partner

began a sophisticated wiggle with his hips.

Kimberly laughed. "No, please, can't we rest now?"

The guy laughed. "Kimberly! I'm surprised," he joked. "You're actually forfeiting the Rock 'til you Drop contest?"

Kimberly held up her hands as if she were praying. "Please, please, don't make me take another step. My feet feel like squashed tomatoes."

He grabbed her hand and wrapped his arm around her waist. It felt warm. Exciting. The attraction between them was like the music. It just kept gearing up, getting hotter, and dazzling Kimberly with its unpredictable beats.

He pushed his way through the dancing crowd, not caring whether or not he had to shove as he led Kimberly out of the gym. Outside, the night sky was cool. Stars hung like sequins on an evening gown. Fireflies punctuated the darkness. The newly cut grass scented the air.

"Wow, Kimberly!" the guy exclaimed. "When I met you this afternoon, you didn't tell me you could dance like an onion in hot oil."

Kimberly laughed and squeezed his hand. "Is that supposed to be a compliment?"

"Most definitely."

"And, uh, Mr. Poetry in Motion," Kimberly teased. "Now that I've danced with you for a couple of hours, would you mind telling me your name?"

The guy grinned. "I'm Clark Kent. I've got a second name that begins with an S, but I can't tell you what it is."

Kimberly moaned. "Aw, come on."

He let out one of his belly laughs. Then his expression turned serious. The intensity of his piercing brown eyes reminded Kimberly of someone she was sure she knew somehow, somewhere. "Okay," he said. "My name is—"

"Oh, wow!" Courtney bounded across the grass, trailing pink chiffon.

The guy made a face only Kimberly could see, then turned on a fake smile and faced the person who interrupted them.

"I'm Courtney Conner, the president of the Tri Beta sorority," Courtney introduced herself. "I can't believe it! It's such an honor to meet you."

Courtney reached out and shook Kimberly's partner's hand vigorously. He began to sway as if Courtney were shaking his arm off. Kimberly put her hand to her mouth, hiding a giggle. It was funny. It was also sort of rude to Courtney.

"Well, I'm sure it *is* an honor for you," Kimberly's dance partner said snidely.

Kimberly smiled at Courtney, wishing at the same time that she'd just go away. She liked the

Tri Beta president, but she wanted to be alone with this incredible guy. Two was company, and three was definitely a crowd.

And five was just plain ridiculous! Kimberly had just spotted an Asian woman in a straight, conservative skirt and another girl with auburn hair and a velvet hairband peeking out from behind a forsythia bush. She recognized them from her visit to Tri Beta House. They'd been the ones giggling when she had spoken to the group. Courtney didn't seem aware of the fact that they were spying on her.

"It's just so fabulous that you could make it to Springfield for UNITY," Courtney went on.

Feeling uncomfortable, Kimberly watched Courtney and the guy. Why didn't Courtney leave them alone? Worse yet, why did the sorority president seem to know so much more about her dance partner than she herself did?

The guy threw Courtney a phony grin. "You're a fan."

"Oh, yes!" Courtney said effusively. "I was flipping through the channels one night, and I saw you interviewed on *The Writers' Corner*. That's how I recognized you."

"And . . . have you read my work?"

The sarcastic possibility that she hadn't went right over Courtney's head. "Absolutely. It's so—moving."

"Moving. Yes." He threw a look at Kimberly as if to say, "This girl is really stupid."

Kimberly wasn't sure how to react, so she looked away. Courtney was amazingly unaware that she was interrupting. Still, Kimberly thought, she and the other sorority girls got a bum deal. A lot of people thought they were a bunch of bubble-head clones. From hanging out with them over the past few days, Kimberly knew that wasn't true. At least some of them weren't. Kimberly wasn't crazy about Diane and Marcia, who were still glaring at them from behind the forsythia bush.

"I—hope I'm not too forward if I ask a favor," Courtney went on.

"Perhaps." Kimberly's dance partner waved his hand in the air. "But go ahead, anyway."

Kimberly was getting a weird feeling, like the time when there'd been that explosion in the chemistry lab and she realized *she'd* been the one who'd mixed the wrong chemicals together. Who was this guy she'd been dancing with all night long? Someone very important, clearly. Definitely a writer. He'd probably been invited to the university for UNITY Week.

"Um . . . " Courtney said. "Would—would you accept an invitation to read your poetry at the Tri Beta sorority house? It would be such an honor, and a pleasure, to have you there."

Wait a second. Poetry? Kimberly stared hard at her partner's face. The high cheekbones, the rounded lips, and piercing brown eyes. Could he really be . . . ? She barely dared even to think the answer.

Courtney caught her breath. "Oh, Mr. Santoya, I know you probably always get a fee for reading. That's no problem. Just tell me the amount, and I'll arrange for it."

Kimberly's mouth dropped open. Rico Santoya! She gaped at him. He laughed and winked at her.

He turned back to Courtney. "Okay, I'll do the reading. When do you want me?"

Courtney considered, ticking off the days on her fingers. "Not early in the week. We can't have a reading until after the living room is finished being painted on Thursday. Friday's the finale of the Futures of Film Festival. And Saturday night is the outdoor jazz concert. Could you do it on Sunday evening?"

Rico threw Courtney the okay sign. "I'll be there."

Courtney grabbed his hand and shook it again. "Oh, that's wonderful, Mr. Santoya. Thank you so much!" She smiled at both of them, then turned and moved across the lawn back toward the dance. Her pink chiffon dress glowed ghostlike in the half-light. Two shadows disengaged themselves from the forsythia bush and hurried along behind her. The three Tri Betas disappeared into the gym.

"Wow, that little sorority queen has a powerful handshake," Rico teased, rubbing his arm.

"She's really a very nice person," Kimberly said.

Suddenly she felt shy. This was Rico Santoya, the famous poet, she'd been dancing with all night, holding in her arms, laughing and joking with.

"So . . . now you know my name," Rico said. He pulled Kimberly close, holding her with both hands around her waist.

Kimberly gasped. It had been exciting being with Rico when he'd just been some nameless mystery man, but now she felt giddy.

"I-I can't believe I didn't recognize you," she said. "You don't look anything like the photo on the back of your book." She visualized the dreadlocks and scruffy beard, then gazed at Rico's neat, wavy hair and smooth cheeks.

Rico waved his hand. "That picture's over a year old. The image was getting stale, you know? Anyway, the new look makes me fit in a lot better at this lily-white, suburban college." He laughed.

Kimberly tried not to let Rico's newly revealed identity make her feel less natural with him. "Give us a break," she said. "U of S isn't so bad."

Rico smirked. "Come on, Kimberly. This place is

like Disneyland without the elves. In Springfield the world is perfect. No hunger. No homelessness. No racism. Just don't step outside the town limits, or the real world might blow your mind. I mean, come on, I just agreed to read my poetry for a bunch of sorority girls in pink tulle."

"It's chiffon," Kimberly corrected.

"Whatever. It still looks like curtain material to me." He swung Kimberly in a circle. "How do you think they'll respond to my poems?" He stared her in the face and quoted:

> *"They found Tito dead on Avenue C*
> *A Spanish prayer spilling*
> *Like blood from his still warm lips."*

Kimberly breathed in, inhaling the smell of Rico's aftershave and the sound of his poetry.

"Anyway," Rico went on, "at least I found you." He ran one finger over Kimberly's lips. "If I hadn't, I would have packed up my bags and flown straight back to the Bronx."

"You wouldn't."

Rico nodded. "I would. There's no way I'd stay locked up in this ivory tower all alone, like Rapunzel from the fairy tale. Not since I cut my dreadlocks," he joked.

"Well, then I guess I'm your prince, come to sweep you off to freedom," Kimberly teased. She snuggled close. Music floated faintly out of the gym.

"That you are, that you are," Rico said. He paused, then kissed her cheek. "So, how about showing me around this town?" he asked. "There's got to be somewhere within fifty miles of this place that's got some grit, some realness. Otherwise, the whole town would just float off the face of the planet like a helium balloon."

Kimberly grinned. She wasn't sure what they'd find to turn Rico's idea of Springfield around, but it didn't matter. The date couldn't be anything but magnificent—at least for her.

"I'd love to show you around, Rico." The name flowed off her tongue like honey. "I've got to get back to the dance now, though. How about tomorrow?"

"Perfect. What's your number? "

Rico pulled a pen out of his back pocket, and as Kimberly reeled off her number, he jotted it down on the back of his hand. Then he walked her back to the gym. At the door he leaned close and let his lips just slightly brush against Kimberly's. Then he sped off into the night.

Eight

Fwhammmm. The handball hit the backboard and rebounded with lightning speed toward Cody.

Fwhapppppppp. Cody sent the ball flying back at the wall. It felt good to work up a sweat, stretch his muscles, and cream his friends. That was what handball was all about.

Dash missed it. "Darn!"

"One more point, then Josh and I win!" Cody crowed.

Brooks snagged the ball, threw it in the air, and sent it sailing back toward the wall. *Flhammmm.* "So anyway," he gasped as he ran, "as I was saying . . ."

Fwhappp. "ROTC's turned out to be different than I thought."

"How so?" Dash asked. *Frrhappp.*

"It's not as macho as I thought." *Fhramm.* "There's a lot of discipline to it." *Fwhammmmmm.* "It's really helping me get my life back in order." *Fllllllap.*

Cody and Josh were about to win the game, no thanks to Josh, though. But Cody was playing like dynamite. Dash and Brooks were too busy talking. And besides, they'd both been out late the night before at the One World Dance. The consolation prize to taking KC home early was that he was well rested for this friendly little Sunday game of killer handball.

Cody dove for the ball. It rolled off the tips of his fingers and went shooting toward the backboard. *SLAM!*

"Game!" he exclaimed as the ball flew like a bullet across the court. It bounced against the far wall and rebounded. Cody caught it in midair and held it up in victory. Josh whooped.

"Wow, that was a great last shot, Cody," Dash said.

"It pays to keep in shape, Ramirez," Cody joked.

Brooks grabbed his towel from the sidelines, wiped the sweat from his face, then slung the towel around his neck. Around them, the shouts of other handball players echoed off the backboards. The four boys gathered up their gear, pushed into the corridor outside the courts, and headed for the showers. Four pairs of sneakers squeaked on the linoleum floor. The UNITY posters that had lined the corridor walls the previous night for the One World Dance had already been pulled down. A few lay torn on the ground.

"So what do you think?" Dash asked Brooks. "Is there any bite behind this rumor about Buck Sandler and Sarah Hunter? Do you really think he's harassing the ROTC girls?"

Brooks shrugged and looked sheepish. "Well, I did hear Buck and Sarah talking behind the girls' locker room. Buck wasn't even supposed to be there in the first place."

"Sounds bad," Cody commented.

"Really," Josh agreed.

Dash shook his head. "If it *is* happening, it's really terrible. But I also know that rumors have a way of getting out of hand, fast. Until I find out a little more about it, I'm still going to keep my eyes and ears open for other story possibilities."

"You're still on the outs with Lauren, huh?" Brooks asked.

Dash opened his hands and shrugged.

Cody could really feel for the guy. Dash had been trying for a long time to rekindle a little love and affection in Lauren. But it was beginning to look hopeless—at least to all of his friends. Still, Dash didn't give up. You had to admire his persistence and deep, true feelings. Cody knew his own feelings could run just as deep. Like with KC, for instance. Now that he realized he loved her, he would be completely devastated if he lost her. But he had faith. Maybe KC wasn't ready to *say* she loved him yet, but he thought she did. It just felt right. Very right.

Cody pushed open the locker room door. Haze curled out of the steam room. A few of the showers were running, and a couple of guys were splashing around and snapping each other with twirled up towels.

"Anyway, I think I've got a lead on another 'His and Hers' story," Dash said. He went to the rows of gleaming sinks and splashed some water on his face. He pulled off his sweaty black T-shirt and slipped out of his sweatpants.

"What kind of story?" Cody asked.

He dashed some water under his armpits and then toweled off. He began changing from his blue cut-off shorts and Tennessee Wetlands T-shirt into jeans and a flannel shirt. He slipped into his vest and started combing his tangled hair into a ponytail.

"You think I'm gonna tell you?" Dash joked.

"You'd probably try and scoop me and get these guys on your radio show." He tossed one of his sneakers at Cody.

Cody ducked. "Hey, give me credit for a little loyalty!"

"Okay, okay. Though actually, I can't really imagine Billy Jones on your show anyway," Dash added.

Cody studied his friend's face. Suddenly Dash looked serious. Troubled even. This must be one special story.

"Anyway," Dash went on, "Until something pans out—either Lauren's ROTC scandal or my own story—we keep on looking. Actually, we're interviewing that visiting poet, Rico Santoya, over at the Beanery this afternoon."

"Wow!" Cody exclaimed.

"Impressive," Josh said. He threw his black leather jacket on over his sweaty green T-shirt with the bleach stain and his ratty cutoff jeans.

Dash grinned, his pride showing through the modest front he was obviously trying to present. "I know. I'm excited. Santoya's work is totally inspiring. And now, I'm actually getting the chance to talk to him in person." He squinted through the steamy air at the big round clock over the sinks. "Whoa, I'm about to be late," he said. I'm supposed to pick him and Lauren up in my new car right about now. Can I give any of you a lift?"

Cody shook his head. "I just have to get over to the radio station."

Josh declined, too. "I brought my motorcycle."

Brooks laughed and shook his head, too. He was just straightening his rugby shirt. "Sorry, I'm supposed to meet my study partner over at the architecture library in a few hours, and I can't afford to get stuck on the road when your engine falls out."

"Hey, are you implying that *El Toro* doesn't work?"

Brooks lifted his hands. "You said it, not me."

Dash threw his other sneaker at him.

The guys gathered up their stuff. "Listen, I really do have to meet my partner at the architecture building," Brooks said. He grabbed his sweaty clothes and ambled toward the door.

Josh went with him. "Thanks for the game," he said with a wave. Then they were gone.

Cody scooped up the handball along with his other gear. Dash retrieved his sneakers and put them in his canvas book bag. Then the two boys headed out of the locker room. Cody tossed the ball in the air and caught it as they walked. Dash's boots clomped against the floor as they walked down the corridor. Toss, catch. *Clunk, clunk.* Toss, catch. *Clunk, clunk.*

Dash stepped close and put his arm around Cody's shoulders. "Hey, you doing all right after last night?" he asked. He sounded concerned

Cody frowned, confused. Toss, catch. "Well, KC is feeling better, if that's what you mean."

After tucking her into bed the night before, he'd gone straight home. That morning before breakfast, he'd stopped off to say hi to her and see how she was doing. She was still in bed, but she'd said she felt much better. He'd tried to get her to go to brunch with him at the dining hall, but she'd gotten all weirded out and sent him off alone. He hadn't thought too much about it at the time. That was just how KC was when she wasn't feeling well.

"Oh, good. Then she didn't flip when she saw Peter."

Peter? For a moment Cody wasn't sure who Dash was talking about. Then it hit him. Peter Dvorsky. KC's ex-boyfriend.

Cody stopped in his tracks. "What are you talking about?" he demanded. He put his hands on his hips, staring in disbelief at Dash. "Peter Dvorsky's supposed to be in Italy. Did he come back to campus?"

Dash took a deep breath. "Oooh, hey. You didn't know."

In fury Cody squeezed the rubber handball as if he could pop it right at the seams. Peter was back. And KC had known it. At least, Dash seemed to think she did.

Relax, Cody told himself. *Play it easy, like you do during a difficult moment on your radio show.* Slowly, he released the pressure on the handball.

"Did—did KC and Peter see each other?" Cody asked. There was an an angry note in his voice.

"I don't know, man," Dash said, wishing he hadn't been the one to give the bad news to Cody. "He—looked pretty anxious to see her. I thought you knew . . ."

Cody ground his teeth, holding back fury, pain, and despair. "And . . . is he planning on seeing her again?"

Dash ran a hand through his hair. He felt miserable. "He's gone now—went to see his family for a few days. He said he'd be back later in the week, though . . ."

Then if he hasn't seen her already, he'll still get his chance, Cody fumed. In a flash of rage, he slammed the handball as hard as he could against the wall. It bounced crazily, as out of control as he felt.

Visions of betrayal flashed through Cody's head like a bad music video. KC had known Peter was around. She'd faked feeling sick so that she could get back to her room and meet him. They'd hung out, talking late into the night. *If* all they did was talk. And that's why KC had been so tired this morning. That's why she'd blown him off for brunch.

"It's just *unbelievable*!" Cody exploded.

"Hey, calm down. Maybe I got it wrong," Dash said. He put a hand on Cody's arm.

Cody pulled away. Why hadn't KC told him her ex was in town? Or . . . maybe he wasn't her ex after all. He'd let himself love her, but she'd never said she was ready to do the same. Because of Peter. Because she still cared for him.

But that wasn't the part that made Cody feel crazy. It was the lying. If KC had only told him, it all would have been all right. He would have known what he was dealing with. He would have figured out how to protect his feelings and his love. He'd fallen in love with KC's intelligence, her beauty, her hidden vulnerability, but most of all, her honesty. He'd thought he could tell her anything and get a straightforward response. Now, he'd found out that was horribly false.

And he was left with his heart on his sleeve and a knife stuck right through it.

Nine

....

Chuggg, chg, cghf. Chg, cghfffff.

Dash's blue, '67 Chevy belched smoke as Dash turned the ignition off in the Beanery parking lot. The smell of burning gasoline filled the midmorning air.

"I *knew* we should have taken my Jeep." Lauren moaned.

"Uh, does your car always do that when you shift into park?" Rico asked.

Dash nodded. "Luckily, *El Toro* has always started right up again—at least so far."

Rico laughed. "*El Toro*, huh? Good name!"

Dash slid out of the wide, leopard print covered

seat of the car. He slammed the door and stepped around the Chevy's polished body, patting the shiny tailfin. Rico liked his car. He'd actually driven around in *El Toro* with him. Dash decided he would never wash the upholstery again.

Rico and Lauren got out, and the three of them headed to the Beanery to finish up their exclusive interview. Rico had insisted on doing the first part of the interview while cruising around Springfield in Dash's car. He'd arranged tutorials with half a dozen U of S aspiring writers at the Beanery later, and he'd said he didn't want to be mobbed by them as the three of them talked.

As Dash pushed open the door, the warm smell of fresh-brewed coffee and cinnamon muffins rose to greet them. Dash grabbed an ashtray from a nearby table and settled in a booth in a quiet corner.

Rico inhaled deeply. "Mmmmm. Feels like home—for the first time since I've gotten to this hick town."

"What do you mean?" Dash signaled to the waiter for three coffees.

Rico dropped onto the hard, polished wooden bench next to Dash. "This place feels, and smells, a lot like the Nueva Yorkian Writers' Café, a place on East Fourth Street where a lot of us poets did our first public readings. I'm surprised to find a café like this in Springfield."

Lauren sat down across from Dash and Rico and immediately began scribbling notes on everything Rico was saying in her pale green stenographer's notebook.

Feeling exhausted, Dash leaned back against the hard, high wooden back of the booth. It was shaping up to be a tough week, with the miscommunication with Lauren, the mad search for a 'His and Hers' topic, the specter of Billy Jones and his creepy skinhead gang, and a million UNITY Week events. And Dash still felt really awful about spilling the news about Peter's visit to Cody.

"You know, they have poetry readings here once a week," Lauren said to Rico. "Too bad you missed the one Friday." The waiter brought over a coffee pot and three cups and and filled them to the brims.

"Not bad at all," Rico contradicted.

"What do you mean?" Dash fished a cigarette out of a crumpled pack, lit up, and offered one to Rico.

Rico held up his hands to say no. "What I mean," he answered, "is that if the readings here feature the kind of wimpy, self-indulgent poetry your English Department sent me as student writing samples, it's an act of mercy that I missed it."

"Oh, come on. We aren't all that bad," Lauren said with a laugh. She was still scribbling notes.

"I wish!" Rico exclaimed. He put one hand on his heart and the back of the other against his forehead in a melodramatic gesture. "'I see the faces passing on the street. They do not see my loneliness. They can not feel my pain!'" he quoted. Then he broke into a deep laugh.

Lauren poured milk in her coffee. "That's only the bad stuff. We've got good writers here, too. I like to think I might be one of them," she said. She looked down shyly into her coffee and stirred it with her spoon.

Rico looked up at the ceiling and shook his head. Dash held his breath. Thank goodness Lauren was too busy playing with her coffee to notice. She would have been really hurt.

Lauren looked up, her violet eyes hopeful and innocent. "Actually, I was wondering if you might be willing take a look at some of my stuff . . ."

This time, it was Rico who stared down into his coffee. "Well . . . I guess I could squeeze one more tutorial in."

"Oh, thank you!" Lauren gasped.

She looked like an excited puppy. Rico, though, acted as if he'd just made a date to have a tooth pulled.

"How about if we meet here on Saturday night, after the jazz concert?" Lauren suggested. "That way I wouldn't take up any of your time during the week. I know you're doing a lot of tutorials and speaking in a number of English classes."

"Okay," Rico said. He let out a little grump, then hunched over, and stared moodily into his coffee.

Dash leaned his elbow on the table and his head on his hand. He stared at the poet intently. In a lot of ways, Rico was just as fascinating and brilliant as he'd imagined. But there was also a distinct arrogant strain in the writer. Rico acted as though he were too good for Springfield, and certainly too good for the crummy poets at U of S.

Should he say something? Hey, why not?

"Uh," Dash began. "You seem a little put out about doing these tutorials."

Rico gave a definitive nod of his head. "You bet I am—no offense, Lauren. It's just that not one single poem I've seen here so far has any grit. And I've still got a week of one-on-ones to do. You're totally cut off from the world here. You may be learning a lot about books, but about life you remain completely innocent."

Lauren had stopped scribbling, half horrified and half entranced by the poet. Then she bent over her notebook and wrote down Rico's speech.

Dash lifted his eyebrows in a challenge. "Okay, so then why did you come here in the first place?"

Rico sighed and leaned on the table with both elbows. His intense face took on a thoughtful, far-away expression. "If you must know, I was curious. I never went to college myself. Secretly, I guess I've always been sort of worried that I was missing something."

"And?" Dash asked.

"And I didn't miss a thing." Rico's tone was hard, even bitter. "You hang around your picture-perfect mountain town, untouched by the real problems and struggles of the world."

"That's not fair," Lauren said in a small, hurt voice.

"But it's true," Rico insisted. "The biggest sign of social strife around here is when the junior study nerd doesn't make the honor role. Springfield has no underside. It's totally unreal. It's totally boring," he finished.

Dash took a long, hard drag of his cigarette, thinking. What would Rico say if he told him about Billy Jones and his vicious band of skinheads? Would racial hate be real enough for Rico? More important, would the worldwise urban poet have some suggestions on how to handle the ugly gang?

Dash stubbed out his cigarette, hesitating just a moment. "Uh, actually, there's something I wanted to tell you about—" he began.

"Excuse me, are you Rico Santoya?"

A tall, blond freshman in safari shorts and hiking boots had walked over to the booth and was staring at Rico eagerly. He had a gigantic stack of notebooks stashed beneath his arm. Hand-scribbled papers stuck out of them at every angle.

"Well, I'm not the Jolly Green Giant," Rico responded.

The eager expression on the boy's face didn't waver. "I'm John Emerson. We have a tutorial now?"

Rico held up his hand. "It can wait." He turned back to Dash. "What were you saying?"

Dash waved his hand. "Never mind, it's not important."

The poet stood up, and took his cup of coffee with him over to a nearby table.

"I'm really excited to show you my work, Mr. Santoya. I've been working on an epic poem about freshman life here at U of S. I've already got over two hundred pages."

Dash saw Rico cringe, then turn on a big, fake grin and pick up one of John's notebooks.

Dash turned back to Lauren. "Well, what do you say?" he asked. It had been exciting being with

Rico, but now the really important part of the interview began—the part where he got to be alone with Lauren.

"I say the interview went *great*!" Lauren answered. She flipped the pages of her steno book. Then she looked away, as if she hadn't meant to be quite so open and friendly with Dash. "But, uh, that doesn't mean I want to write about Rico for 'Hers and His.' The ROTC scandal makes a better story."

Dash waved his hand. "It doesn't matter. I don't want to write about Rico, either."

"You don't?" Lauren gasped.

"Huh-uh. I'm looking into something that could be very important," he said. Billy Jones's leering face flashed across his mind.

"Really?" Lauren looked curious, but she clearly didn't want to ask what, exactly, he was thinking of.

Dash bit his lip. He didn't want to push her away, but he didn't want to tell her about Billy yet, either.

"I can't talk about it right now," he said. He put his hand over hers. It felt warm, gentle.

Lauren slowly, uncertainly, moved her hand out from under Dash's. "Well . . ." she sighed as if she weren't quite sure what to say. "I-I've got to go," she finished. "I've got to finish up a paper."

Dash stood up, hitching up his jeans. "Can I give you a lift back to campus?"

Lauren looked at him for a moment, hesitating. Her face wore an unhappy frown. "I . . . don't think so," she said. She dug into her bag and put some money on the table. "This will cover my coffee and half of Rico's."

Dash dug his fingers into the belt loop of his pants and stared morosely at the floor. He'd hoped the interview with Rico had loosened things up between them. It hadn't, and that made Dash feel sad.

"Well . . ." Lauren rubbed the tip of her round-toed boys' shoes into the gritty café floor. "Bye." She turned to go.

"Lauren . . ." Dash called after her.

She turned, and he saw an expression of sadness on her face. What could he say to make it all work out? How could he bring her right back to his side, into his car, and deep in his heart? Words failed him.

"Lauren, I wondered . . . about that internship."

Lauren twisted her fingers, not looking at him. "They haven't let me know yet. I'll tell you when they do." Then she walked away, pushed open the door, and stepped out of Dash's life again.

Dash drained his coffee cup in a gulp. He waited for the crazy mix of emotions whirling within him to subside. He paid for the coffees, then left the Beanery, feeling let down. He and Lauren had had fun together today. They'd cruised in his car with Rico. They'd even laughed a few times. But that hadn't changed the deep mistrust they felt for each other. Or rather, that Lauren felt for him. Had he betrayed her that horribly? Was there no way to reclaim their love and good feelings?

As for Rico, he'd been fascinating, witty, even wise. But he'd also been self-centered, callous, and closeminded when it came to Springfield and U of S. Dash's image of Rico Santoya would probably never be the same. He'd lost a hero.

Across the parking lot, a few figures were leaning down, peering at *El Toro's* gleaming side. Dash grinned. All over campus, people had been admiring the classic Chevrolet. Then he stopped, and his grin melted into a look of dismay. Those weren't people, they were *skinheads*! And they weren't admiring *El Toro's* finish. Billy Jones and four of his boys were smearing the car with spray paint.

"Hey!" Dash screamed.

Billy glanced over his shoulder, his stubbly, bald head glinting in the sun. He caught one glimpse of Dash and dropped his spray can. His buddies did the same. They took off running. Their military boots crunched on the gravel.

Foreigners Out! the graffiti on the car said. *Kill all N—*. They hadn't finished their messages of hate.

Not stopping to think, Dash took off after them. The nail sticking up from the sole of his boot jabbed into his toe as he ran. His lungs threatened to burst as he pushed himself on, determined to catch up with the hate mongers.

Billy and his gang turned past a gingerbread house that looked straight out of a movie set of a peaceful small town. But there'd be no peace in Springfield with the skinheads running around, Dash thought. He skidded around the corner after them.

A dead-end alley. Five nasty skinheads standing around glaring. A couple of frightened mice scuttling behind overflowing trash cans. And Dash. Alone.

But Dash was too infuriated to think defensively and run. This was the second time Billy and his creepy friends had messed with him. They thought they could just walk all over Springfield, spewing their disgusting messages of hate. And why not? No one seemed to have told them they couldn't. Not the police, not Abraham Allen, who'd been afraid to press charges. And not even Dash himself.

His fury and disgust unleashed themselves in a barrage of words. "What do you creeps think you're doing? You don't belong in Springfield. In fact, you don't belong anywhere. You've totally destroyed the finish on my car with your disgusting graffiti." He glared right at Billy.

Billy glared back. "Oh, so that was *your* car? We thought it was that nigger poet's."

Dash gasped. The casual way Billy used the word made it even more shocking.

"If we'd known, we never would have spray-painted those messages on it," piped up one of the other skinheads. He had a rash of pimples on his cheeks and a snake tattoo on his arm.

"That's right," Billy agreed. "We would have written 'Kill all Spicks!'" He let out a crazy little Woody Woodpecker laugh.

Dash shuddered. "You're nuts," he whispered. "And you're dangerous."

Billy giggled his crazy laugh again. "Hey, we're just protecting our turf. You let one of those uppity guys into Springfield, and pretty soon, we'll be overrun with them."

"That's right!" Pimples yelled.

"Then what do we do for jobs? Houses? Morals?" Billy demanded.

He stepped up to Dash, talking right in his face. Dash could smell onions on his breath.

"Those people, those dark-skinned foreign people," Billy expounded, "they'll ruin everything. Look at what they did to the cities where they live. Crime.

Unemployment. People afraid for their lives, afraid to walk out of their houses. We don't like 'em. And we don't like *you*!"

Dash gagged. The combination of the stale onion smell and Billy's words literally made Dash sick. "If you weren't so dangerous, I'd feel sorry for you," he said. He pointed his finger right in Billy's face. "But since you are, get one thing clear. You mess with me again, you mess with Rico, you mess with anyone I've ever known, talked to, or thought about, and I will track you down. And I will make you one sorry dude. You get me?"

Billy giggled again. "I get you, Mr. Puerto-Rico-the-Beautiful. But you get me. There's a dozen of us in Springfield. And only one of you. So maybe it's you who better start watching his tail, huh?"

Dash took a deep breath. He looked around him. The alley was completely desolate. The five skinheads looked ugly. They looked mean. And they looked like they could easily put him in the hospital for a very long time.

Slowly, Dash took one step backward and out of the alley. Then another. Suddenly he spun on his heels and took off at a run. Billy's high-pitched laugh echoed after him.

Ten

"**W**hat's with Courtney anyway?"

"I don't know. First she drags us all to that One World Dance, where I didn't even feel comfortable wearing my pearls. Now she's inviting that weirdo poet to the house."

"What will she think of next?"

KC sat in the backseat of the Jaguar coupe, listening to Marina and Lisa Jean and cringing. The smell of leather upholstery permeated the air. On the seat next to her was a stack of newly printed fliers for the Rico Santoya reading at Tri Beta on Sunday night. KC was supposed to hand them out outside the student union when she had time between classes.

She twisted her fingers together nervously, not sure whether to answer her sister pledges or agree wholeheartedly with them. They'd just come back from preparing the walls at the sorority house. Or rather, they were *supposed* to have been preparing the walls for painting. Instead, Courtney had announced that the local Red Cross was having a blood drive and she wanted all of them to traipse over there and donate blood. The girls had grumbled, but they'd done it, and the living room walls had remained untouched.

"And then Courtney has the nerve to open up that poetry reading to the whole campus!" Lisa Jean complained as she drove. "Without even consulting the rest of us first," she added.

"The house is going to be a zoo," Marina said.

KC could feel a headache coming on. The girls were right. Courtney was pushing her own agenda on the whole house. But that didn't mean it was right for them to turn on her after she had spent almost three years of total devotion to the sisterhood.

"You know, I don't mind doing *some* of Courtney's good deeds, but she's going overboard. And giving blood is so"—Lisa Jean searched for the right word—"disgusting."

KC felt stretched to the breaking point. With

Cody suddenly declaring his love and Peter showing up on top of it, she needed something stable and sure she could count on. And Tri Beta had always provided that. At least in the past. Now, the sorority seemed to be falling apart just as fast as KC's love life. It wasn't fair. It had to stop.

"Hey, look, Courtney's only trying to do what she thinks is right," KC burst out. "A couple of good deeds might even be a positive thing for Tri Beta."

"Sooooorry," Marina drawled.

"You don't have to get so upset," added Lisa Jean.

KC leaned back against the leather upholstery and stared moodily out the car window. A fat boy was pruning a bush in the campus botanical gardens. A pair of professors ambled slowly, lost deep in discussion.

KC's mind drifted to Peter. Cody and Peter. After she'd run out of the One World Dance, Cody had been really sweet. He'd tucked her into bed, hung around for a while just holding her . . . and when she'd said she needed to sleep, he whispered he loved her and left without a fuss.

Fifteen minutes later, there'd been a knock. Thinking it was Cody, she'd almost gotten up to open the door. Then she heard Peter's voice gently calling her. She froze, one leg out of the bed.

What could she say to Peter? Would she tell him off? Fall into his arms? And if she did, what did that mean for Cody? Kind, generous Cody who was so attentive and who loved her.

KC hadn't known what to do. So she'd done nothing. The knocking had continued for a few minutes. Then it stopped, and she'd heard Peter's footsteps going away. In the days since then, he hadn't come by again. She wasn't sure if he was still on campus. KC didn't know if she was happy she'd missed Peter or sad. Maybe a little of both. And she hadn't seen Cody, either. She'd avoided him.

In the front seat, Marina and Lisa Jean were discussing what to wear during that Thursday night's painting session without looking like total slobs in front of the ODT guys. KC felt glad they'd shut up about Courtney. If people were going to badmouth the Tri Beta president, she, at least, didn't want to listen to it.

Even if they are *partially right,* a little mind in KC's voice chimed. KC sighed and made a forced effort to ignore the thought. Courtney was her friend. Her sorority president. She couldn't have any doubts about her.

Lisa Jean pulled up outside a two-story wooden house with a wide front porch and a big lawn.

"First stop, Langston House," she called from the front seat.

KC gathered up her blazer, attaché case, and textbook on business and finance and pushed open the door. She swung her legs out of the car and got out. The Jaguar roared off, and KC turned toward her dorm. On the porch a guy with a ponytail was swaying slowly in the old rocking chair in the corner. Another guy with brown hair and tight jeans was lounging against the railing, his arms crossed casually over his chest. Cody. And Peter. Together.

KC froze. Cody saw her first. He stopped rocking and just stared at her, his expression hurt and betrayed. Then Peter turned casually over his shoulder and spotted her.

"KC!" Peter called.

He ran over to her and enclosed her in a warm, intimate hug and kissed her right on the lips. Over Peter's shoulder, KC saw Cody stand up in flash of emotion and betrayal. Behind him, the rocking chair went over and clattered onto the floor of the porch.

NO! KC wanted to moan. *Rewind. Replay. Let's do this whole scene over again with a different script.*

After all these months of thinking about Peter, wondering, wanting him, and he had to show up at exactly the same time as Cody. She wanted to enjoy the warm, soft feeling of his arms around her, the gentle caress of his lips. But there was just no way with Cody watching them.

Cody stepped down the two porch steps, his cowboy boots clicking against the wood, and walked across the grass to KC and Peter. KC pushed Peter away gently and stood staring at Cody. What should she say? What could she do to keep him from walking right out of her life for good?

Cody stopped a few feet from them. "Congratulations on the return of your boyfriend, KC," he said. His soft Tennessee drawl was filled with a quiet pain. "You won't have to worry about me getting in the way. Good luck. I hope you two will be happy together."

Then he turned and walked off across the lawn. His long, lean legs ate up the grass as if he couldn't get away from the whole horrible scene fast enough.

Don't go! KC wanted to scream. She wasn't ready to give up Cody, his attentiveness, his long-winded, funny stories, his love. But her tongue froze, and she just watched him leave. He turned the corner and was gone.

Peter pulled KC close again. "KC, it's so good to be with you again." He spoke into her ear, stroking her hair.

KC could feel her body tensing up. If only she could concentrate on the guy who had just walked back into her life instead of the one who had walked out of it.

"I—gather that you and Cody have been . . . involved," Peter said. "That's okay. I was spending time with someone else, too. I think you figured that out, didn't you?"

KC nodded numbly.

"I'm sorry, KC, but I just couldn't be alone for that long. And I guess you couldn't either."

Part of KC wanted to push Peter away. It had hurt so horribly when she'd called his pensione early one morning and discovered he'd been sleeping somewhere else. It was only *after* that that she'd gotten involved with Cody. And now, she could imagine a little bit of what Cody was feeling, seeing the person he loved in the arms of someone else.

But Peter's voice was low, seductive. His hands felt good against her hair and neck. She snuggled against him, letting the good feelings take over.

Peter went on, caressing her, speaking deep into KC's heart. "Ursula didn't really mean anything to me. It was always you I really loved."

Was it? Because KC knew she had always loved Peter.

"My romance with Ursula didn't work out. And

it seems as though your new romance didn't either. It looks to me as though I've come back at just the right time."

KC buried her face in Peter's shoulder, lulled by waves of desire and misery. Maybe he *had* come back at the right time. Maybe he had.

Danny's thin legs stuck out of his plaid shorts and lay limply on the physical therapy table. Before his car accident almost two years ago, he'd had strong, muscular legs that could run from third base and slide into home plate in seconds. Now, he hated the way they looked, so weak and useless. That's why he always wore long pants, except here. So no one would see them.

Lynnie, the physical therapist, picked up one of Danny's legs. She lifted it all the way up and over his head, stretching it beyond what seemed possible. Because he couldn't move his legs himself, he needed superflexibility in order to move them in and out of bed, his wheelchair, a car, or anyplace else he wanted to go. Danny had never had such flexibility before the accident. The only problem was, now he couldn't feel any of it.

"Let's just go through a few more repetitions," Lynnie said. She lifted his other leg.

Lynnie was a physical therapy graduate student at U of S. She had yellow curls and a friendly smile. In a twisted way, Danny actually enjoyed the P.T. sessions with her. It was probably the most physical contact he'd have with a girl, now that he was a paraplegic.

Lynnie laid Danny's leg down on the table. "Okay, pal, that's it," she said. "We did some good work today." She pushed his wheelchair next to the table.

"It's harder on you than on me," Danny joked darkly.

He used his powerful arms to turn himself onto his stomach. Then he lifted himself off the table and maneuvered into the chair. He slipped on his gloves and wheeled himself toward the door. Lynnie gave him a cheery wave as he left.

Sure, Danny thought angrily. *It's easy for her to be cheerful. She can walk to the dining hall, play a game of catch, even get in and out of a car without risking falling flat on her face.*

Sometimes physical therapy made Danny feel upbeat and hopeful. Other times, like today, it just made him hate the world. No matter how much P.T. he did or how hard he worked, he would never be able to get up out of that chair and walk.

Danny wheeled down the hallway, muttering

under his breath. A door at the far end of the hall swung open. A girl with short, fiery red hair, and wearing a Speedo bathing suit stepped into the corridor. She carried a pink bathing cap in one hand. As she walked, she limped—you wouldn't have noticed if you weren't looking hard, but Danny was.

Melissa McDormand! She must be here for one of her own physical therapy sessions, he thought. A lot of the running injuries were treated in the pool. Danny reversed his grip on the wheels of his chair and pushed, trying to make a getaway.

"Hey!" Melissa's voice echoed from the end of the hall.

Danny stopped stock still. No chance to run and hide. Not even a chance to grab a towel and cover his useless legs.

Melissa walked down the hall toward him, swinging her bathing cap. He was painfully aware of her shapely, muscular body in the swimsuit and her powerful, iron-strong runner's legs. Melissa was dynamite. And he knew he'd hurt her.

"Danny. Where've you been?" Melissa asked. She leaned against the wall, one leg crossed casually over the other.

"Oh, just doing a little physical therapy. Got to keep the old legs in tip-top shape, you know?" he said. He waved a gloved hand at his inert legs.

Melissa flicked a look at them. "Yeah, but I mean, before that. Like all week."

Danny stared past Melissa down the empty hallway. "Just busy with classes and schoolwork," he said. He knew she was asking more—like where he'd been on Saturday night instead of the One World Dance.

"Well, I've been busy, too," Melissa said huffily. "But I don't let it get in the way of things I'd planned. With someone I thought was my friend." She bounced her weight from one leg to the other.

Danny tried not to look at those gorgeous legs. And he tried not to think about her looking at his limp ones. That, right there, was the reason he'd stood her up. Because she could walk, run, dance, and he couldn't. Melissa couldn't possibly be seriously interested in him. No girl in her right mind would be. He was a cripple.

At his worst moments, that was how Danny thought of himself. Not paraplegic. Not physically challenged. But a cripple.

"Look, Mel, you didn't really take my so-called invitation to that dance seriously, did you?" he asked.

He had to get rid of Melissa. He liked her too

much. And he knew it could never work out
between them. He was doing them both a favor
by breaking it off early. Maybe if he told himself
that enough times, he'd really believe it.

"Sure I took you seriously. Why shouldn't I?"

Danny faked a concerned looked. "Ah, no, I just
figured you knew I was kidding."

Melissa's expression hardened so that Danny
thought for a moment she was going to shove him
right out of the wheelchair. Then she took a deep
breath and her face relaxed, as if she'd made a con-
certed effort to remain open.

But Danny didn't want her to be open. He
wanted her to go away, so that he wouldn't have
to risk feeling anything for her. So that he
wouldn't have to risk losing her.

"I mean, really," Danny went on. "It's absurd to
think of me at a dance." He let out a sarcastic, bitter laugh. "What did you think we'd do? Wheel
around in circles?"

Melissa's brown eyes blazed into Danny's.
"Actually, Lauren and I had a good time standing
around talking, eating, meeting friends, and
watching people dance," she said.

Danny swallowed hard. Melissa wasn't making
this easy. He forced a hollow laugh. "Listen, I'm
sorry you thought I was really going to show up.

I never intended to. Get the picture?"

Melissa's eyes looked angry for an instant, then suddenly very, very sad. She nodded her head. "Yeah, I do." She turned toward the pool.

A flash of dismay swept over Danny as he watched her go. But it was better this way. Much, much better. He began wheeling his chair in the opposite direction.

"Hey, Danny!"

He wheeled around. Melissa was standing in front of the half-open pool door, her eyes flashing like fire.

"Maybe when you get done feeling so sorry for yourself you can head over to the library and look up the word 'selfish' in the dictionary. While you're at it, try 'arrogant' and 'inconsiderate,' too. Because that's what you were when you stood me up for that dance."

Danny let out an astonished laugh. "Melissa!" he said, making his voice sound surprised at her anger.

"Hey, I mean it," she continued. "I liked you. I took a chance on you. That was hard. I know what it's like to be hurt, too, you know. I know what it's like to try and to fail and then to feel as though no one could ever possibly love me again."

"Melissa . . ." Danny said again, but this time his

voice was soft, pleading. It was too hard to hear Melissa saying these things because then he had to face everything he was ready to throw away.

Melissa shook her finger angrily. "I almost ruined my life wallowing in my self-pity and misery," she told him. "Just like you're ruining yours. Maybe one day, you'll wake up and start thinking about someone other than yourself. Then you'll realize what a jerk you've been. How you dumped your feelings on me. It's all so pointless . . ."

Melissa choked. The anger had turned to tears. As the first one rolled down her cheek, she turned and fled through the pool door.

Feeling stunned, Danny made a slow getaway in his chair.

Eleven

Navaho flute music whistled through the science lecture hall as credits rolled across the film screen. The lights went up for a moment between Futures of Film selections.

"Isn't that Rico Santoya?" Kimberly heard an adoring voice whisper behind her.

"Yes! And who's that gorgeous woman with him?"

Rico rolled his eyes and leaned his head on Kimberly's shoulder. "See what I mean?" he hissed in her ear. "I can't go anywhere without some star-struck groupie attacking me."

Kimberly laughed. A few days ago, she would have thought Rico was being conceited and ungrateful. Now, after spending almost a week with him, she understood. Courtney bugging them at the dance had been only the beginning. Everywhere they went people had attached themselves to him. The groupies hadn't wondered if they'd wanted to be alone.

As the projectionist loaded the next film, Kimberly glanced around the science hall. In the front, Faith, Liza, and Lauren were munching away on popcorn. In the back, Dash was standing alone, looking tense. Everyone else had settled in. A few had even brought along sleeping bags. The Futures of Film Festival was screening twenty-four straight hours of movies and videos. There'd even be a door prize for the viewer who logged the most hours.

The lights dimmed, and images of an Appalachian mining town flashed across the screen. Rico curled his fingers into Kimberly's hair. Kimberly giggled. She had to admit, she hadn't been paying much attention to the Futures of Film selections.

The whispering voices behind them started up again. "I hear Rico's doing a reading at the Tri Beta House on Sunday night," a guy said.

"I'll be there!" a girl hissed.

The voices buzzed like mosquitoes. "Do you think he'll take a look at some of my poetry?"

"Can't hurt to ask him," came the answer.

Rico moaned softly. "No! I can't stand it. If I have to read one more coming-of-age sonnet or confessional ode, I'll lose my mind." He turned to Kimberly and took both her hands in his. "Come on, let's get out of here before those two can bombard me with a semester's worth of bad poetry." He jerked his head toward the whisperers.

Kimberly laughed. "Okay," she said.

"Great. You sneak out first and wait for me outside." He planted a kiss on her lips, then gave her a tiny shove.

Kimberly slid out of her seat, stepped over a few people's knees, then hurried to the door. In the hall, science nerds lounged, taking a break from the library or labs. In a few moments, the lecture room door squeaked open, and Rico stepped out. He had a wild, comically panicked expression on his face.

"Run for it, Kimberly, they're after me," he whispered.

"Who's after you?"

"Old Keats and Wordsworth, sitting behind us." He grabbed Kimberly's hand, laughing, and pulled her toward the main door. Giggling hard, they made it halfway across the lawn before she saw the dark shapes of the would-be poets trailing after them in the night.

"Come on, this way," Rico urged.

He cut through a tree-lined pathway that led away from the main part of the campus. They dashed down the deserted shortcut. They could hear the poets in pursuit. Rico shot off through the bushes, pulling Kimberly down the hill toward off-campus housing. Then he pulled her off the path, and they crouched behind some bushes. In a few moments, their pursuers zipped past them along the path. Kimberly noted that the group seemed to have grown.

"Where'd they go?" Kimberly and Rico heard the guy ask.

Rico let out a quiet laugh. He and Kimberly waited a few minutes, then stood, and began walking down the path again. The tall, pillard houses of Greek Row rose up around them.

Rico guffawed into the night. "What a bunch of jerks!" he said. "For people who are supposed to be so smart, college kids sure can be stupid. People in Springfield are so sheltered, their brains are only working at half speed. Take your Tri Beta girls, for instance."

He motioned toward a squat red building with a big patio. It wasn't Courtney's house, but that obviously didn't matter to Rico.

Rico wore a smug grin. "Do you think those

sorority sisters will really understand my poetry at the reading Sunday night? Not a chance. And that's why I'm not planning to read them any of my poetry after all."

Kimberly gasped. "You mean you're not going to show?"

She had images of Tri Beta House packed with eager students from all over campus and Courtney flying around, trying to wipe some of the egg off her face.

Rico laughed again. "And lose out on that nice fat fee they're paying me? Huh-uh. But I'm going to bone up on my old TV commercial jingles. I can just hear it now—'We're the soda pop generation, feeling free, feeling free.'"

Kimberly stood stock still. "You're not serious," she whispered. "You can't mean you'd really read TV commercials instead of *poetry!*"

Rico gave a sharp nod of his head. "Count on it! No one in that sorority house will even notice the difference."

Kimberly clenched and opened one fist a few times, digging her nails into the palm of her hand. It was mean of Rico. Sure, he was suave, brilliant, sexy, gorgeous, and infinitely hip. But she was also beginning to realize that he could also be snobby, arrogant, and even cruel. He wasn't giving anyone at U of S a chance—except for Kimberly herself.

"Look," she said softly. "Maybe you have good reason to feel superior to the rest of us poor mortals, but I really think you're selling us and all of U of S short."

Rico stepped closer. "Kimberly, please. I never meant you. You're different."

But Kimberly wasn't about to let herself be sidetracked. "Not everything at the university goes smoothly," she said. "I got accused of stealing just because I'm black. A lot of my friends have dealt with incredibly difficult personal problems. It's been tough for plenty of us."

Rico tossed off a superior grin. "That still doesn't mean anyone can write."

Kimberly shook her head, feeling pained. "That's another thing you're wrong on. There *are* good writers here. Wait till you do your tutorial with my friend Lauren Saturday night. She's a great writer."

Rico waved his hand. "Sure, sure."

Annoyance and desire swirled inside Kimberly. Rico was just humoring her. On the other hand, he did seem to like her for real. It was so flattering.

Rico took her in his arms and held her close. His strong stomach muscles flexed against her body. Then he leaned over very, very slowly and brought his lips to hers. It felt as though he kissed her for hours. Days. Right there on Greek Row. Anyone could have seem them. Rico Santoya kissing her, Kimberly Dayton . . .

Gently, Rico pulled away. "Listen, Kimberly, do you know someplace where we can sit together and stare into the shifting wisdom of the night sky? Alone? You and me?"

Kimberly grinned. Any lingering annoyance was swept away. "I can think of just the place," she said.

She put an arm around Rico's strong, slim waist, and they started off toward Mill Pond.

Dash ran down the tree-lined path, glad the damp earth muffled his footsteps. Up ahead of him, Billy Jones and four of his cronies bumbled about in the dark.

"Where'd he go?" one of them asked.

Dash knew. He'd seen Rico and Kimberly cut through the bushes. He knew they had probably hidden behind them. But Billy and his boys hadn't.

Dash had been watching the gang ever since he'd spotted them walking in the door of the science hall. There was no way those skinhead creeps were coming to the Futures of Film Festival to bask in the warmth of multiculturalism and mutual acceptance. There was only one reason Billy and his friends could have shown up. To make trouble.

Actually, Dash thought they'd been making trouble all week. There were a lot of UNITY signs around campus, but there were also a lot of *torn* ones. And his friends on the planning council kept begging him to help them go out and post more up. Dash had a theory Billy and his boys had been tearing them down. And ruining UNITY decorations anywhere they could find them. And stealing equipment. But now they were after people. Real people. Rico and Kimberly.

Billy and the skinheads had gone after Rico and Kimberly when they'd slipped out of the film festival. Dash could just see the headlines: *Poet and College Coed Slain During Racial Incident.*

But now Rico and Kimberly were safe. And Dash didn't want to meet up with Billy and his boys alone. At night. In a secluded place. His meeting with them a few days ago had been scary enough—and was going to put him out a few hundred bucks to get his car repainted. He turned quietly and began sneaking back toward the main part of campus.

Snaap. A branch cracked beneath Dash's boot.

The skinheads turned. "Hey, there he is!"

"It's that foreigner poet."

"Get him!"

Dash took off, but they were too close. Within seconds, the skinheads were upon him. Billy grabbed him by the arm and spun him around. "Hey, you're not the poet," he said.

"No spit," Dash said.

Deep down, he was scared. Very scared. But he knew the way to get hurt in a dangerous situation was to show fear.

Billy squinted into Dash's face. "I know you," he said flatly. "You're that nosy little spick who keeps hassling us."

Dash jutted out his chin and balled up his fists, hoping he looked tougher than he felt. "Don't use that word to me ever again," he said. His voice was low and dangerous.

Billy shoved one of Dash's shoulders. It didn't hurt, but it was definitely meant to provoke. "I'll use whatever words I want, Spick. Now why don't you just tell me why you won't leave me and my good old American boys alone?"

Whoa, keep cool, Dash warned himself.

The skinheads closed in. "You creeps don't know who you're messing with," Dash growled.

"Oh, no? Tell me." Billy shoved Dash's shoulder again.

"My name's Dash Ramirez. I'm a reporter. You touch me one more time, and you'll see your ugly faces plastered all over every paper from here to Los Angeles," Dash exaggerated. "I'll expose every illegal thing you ever even *thought* of doing—from jaywalking to littering."

"Oh, wow, I'm really scared." Billy let out his Woody Woodpecker laugh.

"You oughtta be. You're a sick bunch of losers," Dash lashed out. He was losing it, he realized. But he couldn't help it. They'd goaded him—and it had worked. "The reason you hate so much is because you're so pathetic yourselves."

Billy's face turned red, then purple with rage. This time, the skinhead leader struck out with his fist. It connected solidly with Dash's left cheekbone.

Dash felt his head spin, and pain exploded in his face. Warm blood spurted from his nose and trickled down his chin. The gang closed in. This was it. He was about to be beaten so badly his parents wouldn't even recognize him.

You've got to get away. You've got to escape, Dash told himself. He pressed his lips together, conserving every iota of his strength. Then he lifted his hands and shoved Billy Jones as hard as he could.

The skinhead leader flew backward. "Ooff," he gasped.

The other skinheads stared for an instant. That was all the time Dash needed. He took off through the bushes and down the hill. The skinheads sped after him. He could hear them crashing through the bushes and cursing him.

Run! Dash told himself. He ignored his bursting lungs. At the bottom of the hill, Dash could make out bright lights and houses. If he could only make it there before the skinheads got him . . .

The grass beneath Dash's boots became pavement. The high white columns of sorority and fraternity row beckoned to him like a mirage. Behind him, the skinheads were close. One snatched out at him, but he was just out of reach. He ran until he thought his lungs were going to explode.

Dash sped onto the lawn of the nearest house. Tall white columns rose up around him. Tri Beta House. The building was brightly lit. As he ran across the lawn, he was vaguely aware of people inside, painting the living room.

Behind him, he heard Billy's strange laugh. "The big tough reporter is running off to the sorority girls for help."

Dash wasn't sure he'd get any help from the Tri Beta girls. But he had to get away. He skidded over the lawn and shot toward Tri Beta's back door. Billy lunged for him, grabbing his shirt.

Dash wrenched away and heard a loud ripping sound.

Please be open. Please, he prayed as he took the steps in one leap. He grabbed the doorknob and twisted it. It swung wide. He practically fell inside, slammed the door shut, and slid the bolt closed behind him.

"We'll get you, Ramirez!" Billy Jones's voice taunted from outside.

Dash leaned against the door, his eyes closed, his lungs burning, his chest heaving for breath.

"Dash! What's going on?"

Dash opened his eyes. The long fluorescent bulbs of the Tri Beta kitchen shone down on Courtney. She was standing at one of the huge, industrial stainless steel sinks, washing out paint rollers. He could smell the turpentine.

Dash's eyes bulged. "I'm in trouble," he gasped.

"I can see that," Courtney said.

Suddenly Dash became aware of how he must look. There was blood all over his face. His shirt was ripped to shreds. He stank of sweat and fighting.

Dash and Courtney had an emotion-drenched history. They hadn't seen each other since shortly after he had stood up for her at her sexual harassment case. At the time, they'd resolved to remain friends. Or, at least civil. But how would Courtney react to him now, barging into her house looking like he'd just come out of a street brawl?

Outside, Billy Jones was still howling. "Ramirez, you can't stay in there forever," he yelled. "We'll wait for you to come out, and we'll kill you."

"Please," Dash whispered. "Just let me sneak out the front door. Then, I promise, I'll get out of your way."

Courtney shook her head slowly. "I can't. The living room is packed. The ODT guys are here helping us paint tonight. They'll see you if you go out the front."

Dash's eyes widened. She was going to throw him to that dog pack out there. He was dead meat.

"Come on." Courtney motioned Dash away from the door with one hand. "I'll get you someplace safe."

Dash wanted to throw himself at Courtney's knees in thanks. Instead, he silently followed her. She hurried to a big, wooden door, fiddled with her key ring, and unlocked it. The door swung open. Dash descended the flight of stairs that led to the basement, and safety.

Fwip, fwip, fwip.
Courtney rolled pink paint onto the walls of the

living room along with a dozen other Tri Beta sisters, pledges, and a group of willing ODT brothers. Of course, most of them were doing more flirting than painting, except for KC, who was busy completing a corner of her own, and Annie and Kelly, who were taking care of the left wall. Marcia and Diane, especially, seemed to be slacking off.

"Matt, can you help me?" Lisa Jean whined.

"Hey, Paul, watch it, you're dripping." Marina groaned.

Courtney's mind wasn't on the task at hand. She was worrying about Dash.

When she'd let him in an hour ago, she hadn't dared to lead him right into the middle of the painting party. The girls were already griping about everything she did, from making them all donate blood to the way she brushed her teeth. And other people on Greek Row were beginning to talk, too.

Fwip, fwip.

Poor Dash. Courtney thought of his bloodied face. She hadn't even had a chance to find out what had happened. Some of the girls had started calling for more rollers as soon as she'd let him into the Crypt.

The Crypt was the secret basement room where

the sorority held its members-only chapter meetings. As far as Courtney knew, no non-Tri Beta had stepped foot in there since the construction crew had put the finishing touches on the building seventy years ago. It was totally secret, completely taboo.

And she'd let in Dash. An outsider. A reporter. And one who'd proved with his uncomplimentary pieces on Greek Row and fraternity hazing that he was definitely not sympathetic.

Not that Courtney thought Dash would betray her. But the other Tri Betas must never, ever find out about it.

"Courtney, these rollers are getting gooey again," Cameron said.

"I'll go wash them out," Courtney said. And maybe she'd have a chance to slip down and visit Dash, too.

She collected the used rollers and headed toward the kitchen. As she stepped into the hallway, the Crypt door creaked open. Dash stepped out. He'd wiped the worst of the blood off his face, but in the hour he'd been there, his cheek had swelled up to the size of an orange. It was bright red. He looked as though he'd been hit by a truck.

Courtney gasped, dropped the rollers with a clatter, and rushed over to him.

"Courtney, what's the matter?" KC cried. She hurried into the kitchen, and the Tri Betas and ODTs followed.

Dash stood there, a dazed look on his face. There was a moment of stunned silence as the others surveyed him like a monster from the deep. Then the comments started.

"What's *he* doing here?"

"What's he been up to? Some kind of barroom brawl?"

Then Marcia screamed. She pointed to the Crypt door, swinging open behind Dash. "He's been in the basement. He's been in the Crypt!"

Courtney put her hands over her ears and closed her eyes. They'd been caught. Even KC wouldn't stick up for her this time.

Courtney took a deep breath. She opened her eyes and dropped her hands. "Listen, everybody. Dash was in trouble. I helped him. Please, try to understand."

There was a moment of tense silence. Then Paul Schultz spoke up. "Uh, did you call him Dash?" Courtney nodded mutely. "Not Dash Ramirez, the reporter for the *Journal*." She nodded again.

"Ramirez!" Matt Brunengo exploded. "That's the jerk who wrote the article about ODT's initiation rituals. He deserves anything he gets." Matt moved forward as if he was prepared to punch Dash himself.

Paul and Matt had no right to threaten Dash, Courtney thought, especially not right here in her sorority house. "Hey, leave him alone," she demanded. She waited for the chorus of Tri Betas to back her up. No one did.

"Sorry, Courtney," Paul said, trying to be diplomatic. "But this guy is a threat to the entire Greek system."

"We've got to stick together on this . . . and get rid of him," Matt agreed.

"I'm with the guys," Marcia piped up.

"Me, too," put in Diane.

Paul turned away from Courtney and his not-quite-smile transformed into a grimace. He opened and closed his hands into tight fists. "Listen," he spat at Dash. "You're not wanted here, or anywhere near a fraternity or sorority *ever*."

"Get out of here," Matt growled. "And don't let us catch you on Greek Row again."

Dash threw a shaken look at Courtney. Then he carefully stepped around Paul and Matt, walked through the kitchen and down the hallway leading to the front door.

Twelve

"What a perfect night," Peter whispered in KC's ear.

He leaned back on the picnic blanket and pulled KC close. All afternoon, while KC had struggled over her economics textbook, Peter had waited on the green to get the very best spot for the Saturday outdoor jazz concert. They were sitting right in front of the stage.

Cody's voice blasted through the speakers. "Let's welcome Mr. Guitar Fats and his Memphis Blues Band!"

"Woooh!" screamed to crowd.

"Yeah!"

Shrill whistles rang out in the cool, black night. Students clapped. Crickets chirped. KC stared up at the star-drenched sky, wishing life was just a little simpler.

She should have been having a great time. Her friends were. Faith, Liza, Winnie, and Josh were bouncing and clapping to the music. Kimberly was running around making sure the technical stuff went smoothly. The Tri Betas had spread out several big picnic blankets, put out fresh fruit and sparkling cider, and invited the ODT brothers to join them. The music was a terrific array of fine jazz musicians from New York to California. So why was KC miserable?

"KC, it feels so good to hold you again," Peter said.

"Guitar Fats, it's a pleasure to shake your hand," Cody's voice blared.

Noooo! KC felt like crying. It was just too horrible holding Peter and hearing Cody. In the few days since the scene in front of her dorm, KC had been a total mess. She'd called Cody a dozen times. He was always out—and he hadn't returned the messages she'd left on his answering machine.

Peter, on the other hand, had been around a lot in the past couple of days. They'd hit the dining hall, and he'd brought roses and candles for their table. He'd hung out with her while she studied, taking roll after roll of film of her with her nose buried in *Economic Alternatives*. They'd caught several UNITY events. It had been a real miracle they'd never run into Cody. That would have been just too painful.

But now that nightmare was coming true. For half the night, KC had endured Cody's betrayed stare from the stage. He could hardly miss her and Peter sitting right there in the front. And although KC wanted to cool the physical contact, Peter didn't seem to get her subtle hints. Poor Cody.

Guitar Fats's band adjusted equipment. The crowd quieted down as Fats stepped to the microphone. He began a rocking version of "My Favorite Things." KC wished the music could just whirl her away to some distant, imaginary land. Then she wouldn't have to choose between Cody and Peter. Peter and Cody.

KC rolled away from Peter and sat up. She stared at Cody onstage. He was standing in the wings of the portable stage, right behind a gigantic bank of speakers. He was listening to Guitar Fats—and looking right at her. For a second, their eyes met.

Peter wriggled closer to KC and slid his leg over hers. KC threw him a forced smile and scooted a little nearer to the edge of the blanket.

Why didn't Peter see that she wanted some space? She watched Cody give a sad shake of his head, then purposely turn his back to them. He didn't want to watch. And KC couldn't blame him. She was totally uncomfortable herself.

Uncomfortable. That was exactly the word to describe her feelings about the past few days with Peter. Sure, they'd done all the old, romantic things. But it just hadn't felt the same. They'd tried hard. Maybe that's why every move they made felt false and stilted.

Guitar Fats's music wailed into the night, telling of loneliness, dashed dreams, and people left behind. KC studied Peter. It was over between them, she realized. It had been for ages. It was sad. She had loved Peter. Maybe a piece of her always would. But their magic was in the past now. All the trying in the world wouldn't bring it back.

As Guitar Fats finished his last song, the crowd broke into cheers and happy whoops. The musicians headed toward the wings, and Cody came out to thank Fats.

KC watched Cody's warm, easygoing, totally sincere smile, his graceful, rolling long-legged walk. Cody was the one who made her heart pound. He was the person who brought magic into her life.

But how could she win him back when he wouldn't even look at her?

Dwoooo-eeeeeee! sang the saxophone.

"Shake it!" Winnie screamed to Liza, who was doing a wild shimmy with her shoulders.

Melissa stood slightly off to the side, watching Winnie, Liza, Faith, and Josh boogie to the music. It felt good to be with friends. Everyone was having a great time. She only wished she could dance and jump around with the rest of them. But all that was out until her leg healed. If it healed . . .

She flexed her right leg. There was a dull throbbing in her Achilles tendon. She sighed and settled down in the grass. The saxophonist blew his final chorus, and Melissa's friends flopped down next to her, sweating and exhausted.

"Great show!" Winnie gasped.

"You said it," Josh agreed.

"Kimberly and the rest of the UNITY committee really worked their tails off on these events," Faith said. She rolled onto her stomach and propped her chin up in her hands.

"Where *is* Kim, anyway?" Liza boomed.

Melissa waved her hand toward the stage. "She's running around keeping a dozen temperamental artists from throwing fits," she said. "I saw her earlier, though, cuddling up with Rico Santoya under a tree."

"Whooo-eee!" whooped Liza.

"Totally romantic." Winnie sighed.

Melissa couldn't agree more. It must be great having a guy you really liked—and doubly thrilling if he was as brilliant and famous as Rico Santoya. Of course, right now, Melissa would have been satisfied with the plain old, garden variety college freshman. But every time she began to open herself up to a guy—Brooks, then Danny—they turned around and slammed the door right in her face.

When Danny had given her the blow-off a few days ago, she'd been furious. Then, the anger had mellowed, and she realized that underneath it all, she was really just hurt.

But at least she hadn't totally fallen apart, the way she had after Brooks had left her at the altar. The past few days had been tough. She'd done her share of crying. But she'd kept going to classes and UNITY events, taking care of her leg, and seeing friends. It was a step forward.

The audience danced wildly or sat on blankets, their attention totally focused on the music. Some people chatted or ate picnic food. Half the campus had to be there, Melissa decided. And the half that wasn't had really missed out.

"So where is Rico anyway?" Liza demanded loudly. "Why isn't he with Kimberly this very second?"

"I think he had to leave early," Faith explained.

"Yeah, he's meeting Lauren at the Beanery to take a look at some of her writing," Melissa said. "I don't think Lauren realized the concert wouldn't get started till so late."

"Ooh, how exciting," Winnie squealed. She rolled onto her back and began doing some leg exercises on an imaginary, upside-down bicycle.

"Do you think he'll like her writing?" Melissa asked.

"How could he not? Lauren's stuff is great," Faith said. "Maybe he'll help her get published!"

Melissa couldn't think of anything more wonderful. Lauren was totally dedicated to writing. Melissa only wished her own future looked just as rosy.

"I can't wait to hear Rico read," Faith said.

"I know! Tomorrow night," Winnie said. She continued to bicycle.

"I didn't know the Tri Beta girls socialized with us lowly, mortal dorm dwellers." Josh laughed.

The music wailed into the night. Bodies sweated and danced. Faith nudged Melissa. She twisted around. Her friend nodded with her chin toward the edge of the crowd. At first, Melissa couldn't see what Faith was pointing at. Then, through the dancing legs and milling crowd, she spotted Danny. He was sitting in his chair at the edge of the audience, staring at her. Their eyes met, and he threw her a small, hopeful smile. He waved one hand for her to come over. He couldn't navigate his chair through the crowd.

What was he doing moping around her? Melissa thought. *She* wasn't the one who'd put up the huge red Stop sign for their romance. She was about to turn her back and ignore him. Then she stopped.

Hold on, Mel, she told herself. Whenever she got angry these days, she tried to take a good hard look at what was underneath it. Usually, it was sadness and pain.

Sure. That was exactly what she felt when she thought about Danny. Sadness that they wouldn't have a chance to get to know each other. Pain that he'd said goodbye.

Pressing her lips together so they wouldn't tremble, she stood up. "Good luck," Faith whispered. Melissa squeezed through the crowd toward Danny. She held onto the sound of the music pouring off the stage as if it could help her walk the tough few yards to his chair.

Melissa stepped up to the wheelchair. She looked

down at Danny. "Well," she said, "after that scene outside the physical therapy rooms, I assumed we'd never talk again."

Danny stared her straight in the eye. His gaze never wavered. "I guess that's what I meant for you to think. I wanted to scare you off."

Melissa swallowed the lump in her throat. "So?" she asked.

"So I've been thinking about it. And I realized I was wrong."

"Well," she said, "if you wanted to get rid of me, you could have done it with a little more consideration."

Danny shook his head. "No, that's not what I mean. What was wrong was pushing you away in the first place."

He reached up and took Melissa's hand. For an instant, she felt like snatching it away. Then she looked around at the crowd. No one was watching them. No one cared. She could scream at Danny or give him a chance, but it was totally her own choice. She let her hand lie in his.

"Melissa, I'm sorry. I sincerely hope you can forgive me," Danny went on. "Meeting you has been hard—really hard. I haven't been close with a girl since before the accident. Sometimes I think it's just not possible. I mean, what could a strong, healthy person like you see in a guy like me?"

Melissa didn't know what to say. Right now, with her Achilles tendon throbbing and her head pounding, she didn't feel particularly strong and healthy. But compared to Danny, she was turning cartwheels.

He stared up into her eyes. "Caring about someone special was just too scary. I figured I was just better off sticking to myself than risking getting hurt by caring and being rejected."

Melissa found herself stroking his hand. She hadn't meant to. It just had happened naturally. "I know a fair bit about that kind of thing myself."

Danny nodded. "I know you do. But it didn't matter. I was sure I could never get close to a nadaplegic again."

Melissa let out a laugh. "A what?"

"A nadaplegic. That's my name for people with full use of their arms and legs. You know—a quadriplegic is paralyzed in four limbs, a paraplegic in two, and a nadaplegic, well, that's for none."

Melissa grinned. "Okay, Danny. So do you think you can accept the friendship of a slightly damaged nadaplegic?"

"Friendship? Hey, I'm talking about a little more than that." He grinned and patted his legs for Melissa to sit down.

Melissa looked at him for a moment, then shrugged. What did she have to lose? Only a whole lot of loneliness and a very heavy chip she'd been carrying around on her shoulder for a long, long time. She settled onto Danny's lap.

"Good," Danny said. He put his arm around her waist. He swayed slightly to the music with his strong upper body. Melissa laughed. "Now that we've got the basics in place," he said, "how about a date tomorrow night?"

Melissa felt her heart thumping. "Do you mean the kind you'll show up at or the kind you won't?"

Danny nuzzled her neck. "The first kind. We could take a little stroll—or wheel as the case may be—and spend a little time at Mill Pond."

Melissa twisted around so she could look into his face. "I've got a better idea. How about if we take in the Rico Santoya poetry reading at the Tri Beta house?"

Danny looked incredulous. "You sure you want to go out in public with me?"

Melissa nodded. "Sure, why not? Join the human race, Danny. You're entitled to enjoy college life as much as anyone else at the school. We'll have fun. You can meet some of my friends, too."

Danny froze for a moment. Then, a slow smile thawed his face. "Yeah, I guess you're right."

"Sure, I am," Melissa said. And she knew she was. She wasn't interested in Danny for his legs. It was his tough, never-die determination and his sense of humor. She could get close to him. She already had. And it didn't even hurt.

Lauren peeked over Rico Santoya's shoulder as he read the final paragraph of her story. "The two huge, rainbow-colored wings on Mary Anne's back fluttered in the breeze," it read. "The gray sky had turned pink with the rays of the setting sun. She flapped into the sky, free."

Lauren watched Rico with timid, hopeful eyes. It was late. The Beanery was practically empty. The kitchen crew was scouring out the espresso machine, which made a horrible sound as clean water pumped through the nozzle. A waiter was piling chairs upside down on the empty tables.

The famous writer stretched, Lauren's story in one hand, then threw it down on the table. It landed in a tiny spill of coffee, which spread around the edge of pages.

"Well?" Lauren asked hesitantly.

"Well . . ." Rico hedged.

Lauren waited. The espresso machine hissed. Rico fiddled. It was a bad sign. If he'd liked her writing, he would have just come out and said so.

Behind them, the waiter called out to somebody. "Excuse me, but we're closing."

"I'm just meeting friends," Kimberly's voice rang out.

"Oh, you're Rico Santoya's friend," the waiter said respectfully. "For him, we stay open all night."

Kimberly hurried over to Rico and Lauren's table. She leaned over, kissed Rico on the cheek, and sat in the seat next to him. "Sorry I'm so late," she gasped, out of breath. "But as you know, the jazz concert ran over."

"It's okay," Lauren said in a small voice.

"I got here late, too," Rico explained. He turned to Lauren. "Look," he said flatly. "You have got to stop falling for those overly romantic descriptions."

"What do you mean?" Lauren asked timidly.

Rico let out a deep laugh. "Like this—'The gray sky had turned pink with the rays of the setting sun.'" His voice dripped with sarcasm. "Hey, tell me something I've never heard before." He leaned back in the booth, looking satisfied with himself.

"Rico . . ." Kimberly said. She put her hand on his arm as if to hold back his words.

Rico turned on her. "Look, she wanted my honest opinion, and I'm giving it to her."

Lauren caught her breath. It hurt. But the worst part of it was, Rico was right. The description was dead, boring. Why hadn't she seen that before?

"But . . . the story idea . . . what did you think?" Lauren stammered. Professor Jacobsen had loved the plot. So had the other students in her advanced creative writing seminar.

Rico waved his hand in the air to dismiss the entire story. "Too sweet. Not enough grit. My advice to you is this—go out and live a little. Until then, you won't have a single real thing to write about."

Lauren could feel tears welling up in her eyes, and she willed them not to spill over. *You will not cry in front of Rico Santoya,* she told herself. But his criticism was devastating.

She gathered up the damp, coffee-stained pages and neatened them into a pile. Should she show him some of her other work? Did she dare? He'd only trash it. But . . . she had to redeem herself. She couldn't walk out with a handful of hurtful comments and a crushed ego.

"I know what you mean about the subject matter," Lauren said. It wasn't totally true, but she knew if she went home and thought about it really hard, she would. "When I first got to U of S, I wrote a lot of stuff that wasn't too hard-edged.

But I've changed. For instance, I'm onto a really important story right now."

She blathered on. Rico looked bored, but she couldn't seem to stop herself. She had to impress him.

"My story's about the ROTC corps on campus. Buck Sandler, a senior cadet leader, has been pressuring freshman cadet Sarah Hunter for sex. It's nasty, and I'm going to blow the whole scandal on the front page of the *Journal*."

"Oh, mmmm, sounds interesting." But Rico seemed more interested in snuggling up to Kimberly than in their conversation. Then, he moved his head sharply and swiveled around. "Wait a second," he said. "What did you say? A senior ROTC cadet and his freshman sweetheart?"

Lauren began to object. Sarah wasn't Buck's sweetheart, she was his victim. But Rico waved away her objections and dug in his bag. He pulled out that day's *Springfield Gazette*. He threw it on the table in the spilled coffee and quickly began flipping through it.

"Aha!" he said, pointing triumphantly to a small item in the middle of one of the back pages. "Read that!"

Lauren pulled the paper toward her. It was the bridal announcements page, and the small headline was *ROTC Cadets to Wed*. Feeling slightly sick, Lauren read.

> ROTC cadets Sarah Hunter and Buck Sandler will marry next week. The two met in the air force prep program and quickly fell in love. But their relationship was forbidden by ROTC rules, leading their superiors to warn them either to desist from seeing each other or leave ROTC. They were given a deadline, which was to have expired next week. Both Sandler and Hunter have already resigned from ROTC.

Lauren stared at the newspaper, stunned.

"See?" Rico crowed. "Even your big scandal turned out to be a bore."

"I . . . didn't realize . . ." Lauren said in a small voice.

She felt as if she'd been kicked in the stomach. Her creative writing was crummy, her journalism was a joke, and for the past week she'd been trying to stick it to Dash with a big scoop that had turned out to be a big nothing. It was ridiculous. She was ridiculous.

But she wouldn't cry. Not now. She gathered up her stories, poems, and articles and shoved them into her bag.

"Thanks for the critique, Mr. Santoya. I learned a lot," she said. Her voice quivered. As she shoved out of the booth, she knocked over Rico's cup, and coffee splattered everywhere. She ran out of the Beanery before he could say anything, before her tears began raining down without end.

"Rico! How could you?" Kimberly demanded.

Rico smiled smugly. "I told her the truth. It's the least I could do for that poor, sheltered college girl." He motioned toward the waiter, who ran over attentively, wiped up the spill, and filled Rico's cup. Rico leaned his head against Kimberly's shoulder. For once, she pulled away.

"You hurt her!" Kimberly scolded. She was furious, disappointed, even shocked. Sure, she'd seen Rico be condescending and self-satisfied all week. But she'd been too charmed and enthralled to care. This time, though, Rico had hurt a friend. "You treated Lauren like dirt! If you'd been a little less arrogant and cruel, maybe she would have had the nerve to show you something else—something you would have liked."

Rico squirmed. "Arrogant? Cruel? I'm not, really."

"Oh, yeah?" Kimberly challenged. "You came to U of S without a shred of respect for anyone here, and you've spent the past week dashing the hopes of dozens of young writers. If you thought you'd hate U of S so much, you should have stayed home."

Rico shook his head, his coffee totally forgotten. "But what else could I say? That story wasn't any good. And her ROTC scandal was just a big joke."

Kimberly glared at him. "You could have figured out a way to let her down more easily. Or is that just too hard an assignment for the great Rico Santoya?"

Rico stared. He seemed shocked, amazed.

Kimberly couldn't stop the words from pouring out. "Rico, you hurt Lauren, you've insulted practically every writer on campus—and if you go to the Tri Beta poetry reading tomorrow and spout fake poetry, I'm going to get up there and shout you down for what you really are. A big phony."

Rico's brown eyes widened. "You wouldn't!"

"Try me!"

Kimberly pushed her way out of the booth. For the second time that night, Rico's coffee went spilling all over the table. Kimberly didn't care. Let it ruin every pair of pants he owned. Rico Santoya didn't deserve better—no matter how brilliant and famous he was. She stormed out of the Beanery leaving Rico alone and, she feverently hoped, humiliated.

Thirteen

Dash flipped frantically though the Springfield telephone book. "Jones, Jones," he muttered to himself. He had to find the skinhead leader—or at least where he lived. Then he could report him to the police for assaulting him. Or at least, keep the group under strict surveillance. He was going to nail those creeps, but good.

It had become a personal vendetta. They'd insulted him, ruined his car, attacked him physically, and threatened his friends and colleagues. He lifted up his hand to probe the huge blue and purple welt that marred his cheek. "Ouch," he gasped.

There were a lot of Joneses in the phone book. There were even two William Joneses. Dash had called them. One was a lawyer, and the other, from the sound of his voice on the phone, was a very old man. Now, he was trying W. Joneses and B. Joneses, of which there were a total of seventeen. He dialed a number.

"Hello?" a woman's voice answered.

"Uh, hi," Dash said nervously. "Is Billy there?"

"You must have a wrong number," the woman said. "No one named Billy lives here."

"Sorry," Dash said and hung up.

It was like that with all the numbers. Sometimes Dash got an answering machine, but it was never Billy's voice on it. By the time he came to the end of his list, he was beginning to feel desperate. Billy wasn't in the phone book. At least, not under his own name. Dash checked the business section of the book and flipped to *Y*. There was no Youth for a Pure America listed, either.

Dash buried his head in his hands and ran his fingers through his black hair. He'd bombed out. Billy and his gang were out there, but Dash had no idea where. The best he could hope for now was to run into them in yet another dark, secluded place. *Yeah, right,* Dash moaned. *You need that like you need another black eye.*

He needed advice. If he went to the police without a concrete lead, they'd just fill out some forms and bury the case. Greg Sukamaki? The *Journal* editor might have some good ideas, and as an Asian, he had a personal stake in smashing the racist gang. Dash got up, grabbing his list of notes, and started for the door. Then he stopped. On the other hand, Greg might just as soon order Dash to get some hard information before he came around bothering him. Greg could be real tough.

Dash sank back onto the battered, torn old cushion on the seat of his work chair. He thought about calling Abraham Allen. His fellow skinhead victim would definitely give him plenty of emotional support. But Abraham had also made it quite clear he didn't want to get involved in prosecuting, investigating, or in anyway messing with the skinheads.

Lauren! Dash thought. She was the person he *really* wanted to talk to. She'd always been there for him during the worst—when they'd investigated the vicious fraternity hazing, when they'd done the piece on the Springfield food pantry. So what if they'd been fighting lately? When he told her about the skinheads, things would be different. She'd see how important this was. She'd want to help him. Quickly, he dialed her number.

Lauren picked up on the third ring. "Hello?"

Suddenly, Dash was nervous. "Uh, hi, Lauren? This is Dash." For a moment, there was silence on the other end. Dash tugged on the curly phone cord.

Then, in a dull voice, Lauren said. "Oh, it's you."

Dash ignored her tone. "Look, Lauren, I'm onto a story. A very important story. I need your help."

"Um, I'm kind of busy now. I'm on my way to the Rico Santoya reading at Tri Beta."

Dash bit his lip. "This is big. Really big."

There was more silence. In a flash, Dash realized he'd gone about this all wrong. Lauren must be insulted. He'd totally ignored her ROTC story, as though it wasn't important at all. He acted quickly, hoping to smooth things over.

"Listen," Dash hurried on, "I know you're onto this ROTC thing. If you help me with this, maybe we can go over to the ROTC grounds and do a little more snooping later."

He held his breath, hoping she'd say yes. He needed Lauren. She was smart, tough-minded, and unafraid to dig into the most seamy and dangerous story. Together, they'd pull the sheet off those Ku Klux Klan, Nazi skinheads. Together, they'd share the glory.

On the other end of the phone, Lauren gave a choked little cough. "Look, I've run into a little problem with my ROTC story," she said.

"Great!" Dash answered. "Then we can concentrate on my angle."

Lauren blew up. "I should have known you'd take that attitude! You were never into my ROTC story in the first place. Now you're glad I've made a total fool of myself."

"Wait, Lauren, hold on," Dash said, trying to calm her. He'd pushed a button, that was for sure, but he wasn't quite sure why.

But Lauren wasn't listening. "Do your own research, Dash. I don't want any part in it," she yelled.

The sound of the telephone receiver being banged into the cradle resounded painfully through Dash's head. He'd blown it. He'd totally alienated Lauren, and he had nothing on Billy. Springfield was in danger, and his life was a mess. He turned from the phone feeling hopeless. Idly, he flipped through the phone book. F . . . G . . . H. . . . A name caught his eye.

A. Hitler. Could Billy really have dared to list his phone under the name of the Nazi monster? Feeling sick and shaky, Dash dialed the number.

After four rings, an answering machine clicked on. "Hello" came Billy Jones's voice. The machine sounded old and battered, and the tape was scratchy and hard to understand. "You've reached the Springfield chapter of Youth for a Pure America. Leave your message after the beep.

Zeig Heil!" He finished with the Nazi salute.

Paydirt! Dash slammed the phone down and banged his fist onto the open pages of the phone book. He grabbed a pen and scrawled out the 27 Olive Street address listed for A. Hitler on the back of a used envelope. Then he slipped on his *San Francisco Chronicle* T-shirt and motorcycle boots and ran out the door. He'd get the skinheads, with or without Lauren's help. He'd scoop her—and every other reporter from here to Denver. Then she'd really be impressed—and sorry that she hadn't gotten in on the story from the start.

If only *El Toro* were waiting for him out front, instead of being laid up for a paint job in the garage, getting the vicious graffiti covered over. Olive Street was a dead-end road in a bad section of town on the other side of campus, at least two miles away. It was going to be a long run.

But Dash was enthusiastic, excited. His hatred for the skinheads gave him a surge of energy as he took off across campus. He passed the science center and Plotsky Fountain. On Greek Row, Tri Beta house was all lit up, and people were starting to arrive for the Rico Santoya reading. Dash craned his neck, looking for Lauren, but he didn't spot her. The houses got crummier and more rundown as Dash got closer and closer to Olive Street.

Dash swallowed the churning, clothes-in-a-washing-machine feeling inside his gut as he crept up to the address. At least he'd taken out the nail that poked through the sole of his boot. His toe still hurt from its earlier gashes, though, but Dash barely noticed . He'd finally tracked down the skinheads.

Twenty-seven Olive Street was a small, one-story house with peeling paint so old it was hard to tell what color the walls were supposed to be. Patchy, diseased-looking stubs of grass dotted what had once been a lawn. In the pitted, rutted gravel driveway sat a rusty green station wagon with one blue door.

The lights were on all over the house. Without curtains in the windows, Dash could see right in. Illuminated by a bare, overhead bulb, Billy and his boys were sitting around in a circle, passing around bottles of what looked like beer. A TV with the sound turned down emitted blue light. There was a big poster of Adolph Hitler and one of a Ku Klux Klan cross burning. There was also a gigantic banner of the snake with the beady eyes and the knife in its mouth—the skinhead emblem.

Dash crept under an open window. A tinny recording of old Nazi marching tunes wafted out. The skinheads' voices rose above it.

"We'll show them," one of the gang members growled.

"Yeah. No one will ever dare to invite some foreign poet to Springfield again."

Rico! They were going to mess with him again, Dash realized. But how?

"And we'll teach those up-tight, liberal sorority girls not to protect some America-bashing spick journalist," a third skinhead spat.

Billy looked around at his boys. His expression was happy, even sublime. "The main chapter in Oregon will be pleased, very pleased, when they find out we've totally destroyed that foreigner-loving sorority house. We might even get a few casualties this time." Billy let out his high-pitched laugh.

Wait! Dash thought. *Totally destroy Tri Beta House?*

He poked his head up a few inches to peek in. *Hold on!* he wanted to shout. Those weren't bottles of beer the skinheads were passing around: they were empty bottles that the Youth for a Pure America were filling with gasoline from a couple of big, metal cans.

Billy held up his gasoline firebomb and shook it. "First we soak the area around the sorority with gasoline. Then we throw some of these through the window and *kabloom!* The whole place goes up like a toasted marshmallow."

Dash stared, unable to take his eyes from the sloshing gasoline firebombs. It was impossible, sick, insane.

Dozens of people, maybe even hundreds, would be at Tri Beta House tonight. It the skinheads lobbed those firebombs into the house, it would be a massacre.

Lauren! Dash realized. She was planning to go to the reading. Maybe she was even there already. And she'd be there when Billy and his thugs tossed those bottles of flaming gasoline through the windows.

"Okay, boys, come on," Billy ordered. "*Zeig Heil.*"

"*Heil!*" the skinheads shouted as they shot their right arms up in the air for the Nazi salute.

Billy motioned with his hand, and the skinheads got up and began lugging cans of gasoline, the firebombs, old rags, and other tools of destruction toward the door. Dash ducked away from the window and faded into the shadows. He didn't wait to watch the gang load their gear into the rusty green station wagon.

I've got to get out of here, Dash realized. *I've got to get to Tri Beta House before the skinheads do.* It was the only way to save the sorority house, his friends, Lauren. But the skinheads were traveling by car, and Dash had only his feet . . .

It was going to be a long run back to Tri Beta. Desperation and sweaty fear fueled Dash. He shot out of the shadows and careened down the street toward Greek Row.

Fourteen

elcome to Tri Beta House," Courtney said.

"Welcome to the reading," Kimberly said.

Kimberly and Courtney stood by the door, ushering in the hoards of people who had come to hear Rico read. The chairs filling the Tri Beta living room were already taken, and students, teachers, and curious townies had begun to line the staircase and cram into the back for standing-room views.

"Sorry, there are no more seats, but you can stand in the back," Courtney told a few new arrivals. They pushed inside eagerly.

Courtney was charging two dollars admission. All the money would be donated to the Springfield soup kitchen, and the sorority itself was coming up with Rico's fee. Kimberly had heard that some of the girls had put up a real stink about that, but Courtney had won out in the end.

The mood was upbeat and excited, but Kimberly felt an odd darkness in the air. KC and Cody were both there, but they were sitting in different corners of the living room and making a big deal about not looking at each other. Peter was nowhere in sight. Lauren was sitting in a chair at the back of the living room and moping. And a group of ODT brothers had taken up positions near the door, the better to flirt with the Tri Beta girls. When Rico saw the laughing, flirting students, he was going to throw a fit.

Who cares what Rico thinks? Kimberly thought angrily. *He ought to be worrying about what I think.* Would he be arrogant enough to go through with his threat to shout television jingles at this excited group of people? She wondered what the "great man" was thinking in Tri Beta's upstairs sitting room, where he was preparing for the reading. Was he planning to make a joke out of Courtney, the Tri Betas, and every single person here?

"Welcome to the reading," Kimberly said to a

blond guy in a wheelchair who had stopped just below the three low steps leading up to the Tri Beta porch. Then she noticed Melissa standing beside him. Melissa was wearing a pretty red dress and a white cardigan. Kimberly noted that Melissa was wearing a subtle bit of makeup. She smiled and said hi.

Courtney hurried over, a worried, everything-has-to-be-perfect expression on her face. "You'll need help getting up the stairs," she said to the blond boy. "Matt, Paul, and some of the ODT brothers can lift you."

"That's not necessary," the boy said, shaking his head. "All I need is a wide plank. Lay it across the steps, and I can wheel myself up the stairs on my own."

"Hmm," Courtney murmured, thinking. "Unfortunately, it's easier for the guys to lift you than for us to find a board right now." She motioned Matt and Paul over.

As the fraternity brothers leaned down to lift the chair, Melissa's friend made a face. "This is the part I hate the most," he muttered softly. "Feeling helpless."

The two of them paid their admission and moved inside. Kimberly ushered Danny to the front of the room, the only place left with enough room for a wheelchair. Melissa gave him a wave, then squeezed in at the back, with the other standing-room guests.

Wow, talk about a success, Kimberly thought. The Tri Beta reading was really packing them in. In fact, it was packing *too many* in. Kimberly pushed her way toward Courtney just as another wave of people swarmed up to the door.

"Courtney, there's no room," Kimberly called across the crowd. "We're going to have to turn them away."

"Just what I was thinking," Courtney agreed.

Kimberly spotted Faith, Winnie, Josh, Clifford, and a few other of their friends in the group outside the door. Faith waved. Kimberly felt terrible. Her friends—and plenty of others—were going to be so disappointed.

But, a tiny voice reminded Kimberly, *not as disappointed as the people inside if Rico fakes the poetry reading. He better not. He just better not.*

Courtney stepped to the front of the Tri Beta porch. She waved her hands, calling for attention. "People, I'm very sorry, but there are no more seats. There isn't even any more standing room space."

A moan of disappointment went through the crowd outside.

Just then Kimberly heard applause inside. She turned. Rico had just descended the staircase.

Kimberly pushed through the crowd and up to the front, where she'd saved herself a seat. She had to admit, Rico had never looked better. His black jeans fit his slim, long legs like a glove, and his sleeveless black T-shirt showed off the gorgeous muscles of his strong arms.

Rico glanced toward Kimberly and gave her a sheepish shrug. Kimberly could feel the old attraction tugging at her. *We'll just see,* she thought, cutting off the flood of emotions, *whether he reads poetry or garbage.* If it was garbage, then Rico was just a jerk and a joke. And that meant their whole romance had been a joke, too.

Courtney squeezed to the front to introduce Rico. "Hello, everyone. I know you've been waiting a long time, but I finally have the pleasure of presenting Rico Santoya!"

Whistles and exclamations rang through the sorority house. Kimberly leaned back in her chair, crossed her arms over her chest, and glared. Rico opened a battered notebook and took a deep breath.

"This is a poem I wrote just yesterday," he said, his voice booming over the crowd. "It's for a special friend. She's in the audience tonight." He glanced at the page before him, then closed his eyes and began to recite.

> *"I walked with her.*
> *Graceful.*
> *Like the wind across campus.*

> *She told me things had changed I*
> *didn't believe her*
> *until I*
> *looked into the deep, empty hollow*
> *of my heart."*

The audience clapped and shouted their approval. Rico opened his eyes. He looked right at Kimberly. There were tears in her eyes. He'd written a poem. A real poem. For her. All for her.

Dash felt as though his lungs would burst, but he kept running. The gash on his foot from the nail in his boot throbbed, but he ignored it. The skinheads were going to firebomb Tri Beta house, and only he could stop them.

Lauren! his mind screamed. He had to save her. He had to save everyone.

Dash half-ran, half-fell around a corner. The elegant houses of Greek Row loomed before him. He stopped in front of the Tri Beta house. He craned his neck, looking for flames and sniffing the air for smoke. Nothing. The night air was sweet and calm. Clapping floated into the dark from the packed Tri Beta living room. He was in time. Thank God, he was in time.

Dash sped down the street. He had to find the rusty green station wagon with the blue door. Automobiles of every make and color were parked on Greek Row that night. But no skinhead car. Dash turned and ran back toward Tri Beta, checking the cars a second time.

Well, of course, he scolded himself. *They parked it a few blocks away so it couldn't be identified.* But they were around here. Those murderous, horrible skinheads had to be. Dash sneaked around the back of the sorority, toward the door where Courtney had saved his life just a few nights ago. They had to be here.

But there were no skinheads. The night was quiet.

Dash gasped for air. What was going on? He'd heard the skinheads planning their evil night's entertainment. He'd seen the gasoline and firebombs. They'd sped off in the car; he'd run. They had to have gotten here before he did.

Unless . . .

Unless it was all some kind of big, awful joke. They'd seen him sneak up to their house. They'd decided to scare the heck out of him and made up a big story about firebombing the sorority house.

But why? It didn't make sense. If the skinheads had seen him, they just would have beaten him up. Subtlety wasn't their strong point.

Dash careened back toward the front door. He'd ask someone inside if they'd seen anyone. He took the three porch steps in one jump. He pushed open the door. A pretty black sorority sister poked her head out.

"I'm sorry," she whispered. "There's no more room."

Frantic, Dash pushed his way in. "Please, let me explain," he insisted. Then the door swung open a little further, and ODT brother Paul Schultz stepped out.

"The lady told you there's no room," he snarled.

Paul stepped onto the porch with Matt Brunengo right behind him. They pulled the sorority door closed and glared down at Dash.

"What are you doing here?" Paul demanded. "We told you not to show up on Greek Row again."

Dash wasn't scared. The skinheads scared him, not these fraternity brutes. He couldn't seem to get enough air into his exhausted lungs. "They're coming," he gasped. "Jones. His gang. Firebombs. We have to get everyone out."

Paul looked worried for a split second. Then he broke into a sneer. "Good try, Ramirez."

Matt guffawed. "You looked so worried there, I almost believed you for an instant," he said. "But you're just trying to disrupt another Greek event."

Dash waved his hand in the air. "No!" he croaked. "It's true. Please."

Through the open window, he could see the crowds. On the back. Her face looked entranced, transformed.

Dash gasped. "You better listen. Fire. I'm serious."

Paul and Matt stepped forward until their bodies were pressed against Dash. Then they edged him off the porch. Dash fell on his rear on the lawn.

"We mean it. Get out of here. Or we'll hand you a beating you'll never forget," Paul threatened.

"You better listen!" Dash said again.

Paul prodded Dash with his foot. "If you don't get out of here right now, you'll regret it. Now go!"

Dash looked up at the menacing frat brothers. If he wanted to stop the skinheads, getting beaten up by Paul and Matt was not the way to do it. He stumbled to his feet and backed away. Paul and Matt's laughter echoed after him into the night.

Dash didn't care. So they'd humiliated him. Threatened him. Made a fool out of him. But that wouldn't matter if the skinheads showed up. If . . .

Where were they?

Suddenly it all seemed like some mixed-up nightmare. The gang. The bottles of gasoline. The threats. Had Dash dreamed them all up? Or were the skinheads just waiting for the right moment to strike?

*   *   *

Danny let Rico's words wash over him, concentrating less on the poet than the event itself. It was odd being in this big crowd of happy, healthy people. It had been so long. For ages, he had felt too embarrassed to show up at events like this.

Take getting in the door, for instance. If the house had been wheelchair accessible, he would have just wheeled himself inside with dignity and self-assurance. Instead, he'd had to have two strong guys pick him up like a baby. They'd been friendly, but he'd seen their pitying stares. Danny knew he probably would have been just like them, too, if it hadn't been for the accident.

Across the room at the back, Melissa was watching him. She smiled and waved. Danny grinned. Melissa was great, someone really special. He couldn't believe he'd almost chased her out of his life forever.

But he'd taken the chance. He'd put his feelings on the line. And it felt good. Sure, it would be scary. He might find himself at readings, dances, parties. He might have to get carried up a few stairs every so often. He'd have to face his feelings of inferiority. But he wouldn't have to do it alone, and that would make it all worthwhile.

Danny leaned back in his chair, smiling. Then he sniffed a faint burning smell. Burning toast? Dinner left in the oven too long?

The smell got stronger. Danny sat up straight.

Other people were beginning to notice. An uncomfortable hubbub disrupted Rico's poem.

Then something went sailing through the living room window and exploded in flames. Luckily, it caught on the lace drapes. Otherwise, the fire-bomb would have landed smack in the middle of the audience.

"FIRE!" a Tri Beta sister screamed with all her might.

"FIRE, FIRE," the shout ran through the crowd.

People jumped up, toppling chairs, and running for the door. The crowd bottlenecked. People screamed. Others cried. Someone smashed a window and climbed out of it. A terrified group followed. Smoke poured into the living room, making it hard to see. People choked and gagged.

At the front of the room, Danny sat absolutely still. His physical therapists and counselors had always talked to him about situations like this. "Whenever you go anywhere, check out the doors," they'd told him. "Plan an escape route that's wheelchair accessible. Make sure you can get out. In the panic of an emergency, people may forget about you, and you'll have to fend for yourself."

It was happening. He'd been sure it never

would, but he'd been wrong. Danny thought about the three porch steps that stood between him and safety. There'd be no guys to help him get past them now. Maybe there was a back door, but Danny had no idea where it was. Besides, there might be steps there, too.

He was stuck because of three lousy steps. Meanwhile, the Tri Beta house was burning down around him.

The skinheads poured out of the basement of Tri Beta house. "Oh no!" Dash gasped.

From his place in the dark shade of a weeping willow tree at the side of the house, Dash could see a basement window swinging on its hinges. Obviously, the skinheads had forced it and gotten into the sorority house. Dash must have shown up just minutes later. The whole time he'd been running around looking for them and wondering if they'd even show, they'd been inside the place, soaking it with gasoline.

He saw smoke curling out the open basement window. Then he heard a crashing sound. Billy Jones had lobbed a flaming bottle of gasoline at a second-story window. It missed its mark, however, and crashed on the windowsill.

Crashhhhhhhh. From the sound, Dash knew that

one of the skinheads had thrown another firebomb through one of the living room windows. Then Dash heard another.

People poured out onto the lawn, pushing, screaming, and crying. Dash knew there must be scores of people still trapped inside.

It's happening, Dash realized. *The nightmare is coming true!* He had to stop the fire. He had to put it out, before flames enveloped the building, killing dozens.

"Lauren!" he screamed as he took off toward the open basement window and squeezed inside.

A blast of smoke and intense heat hit him square in the face. Nonetheless, he battled his way into the basement. Through the whirling smoke, Dash could make out flames curling up one wall. The fire was still manageable. He could put it out. He pulled off his T-shirt and began beating the flames with it. He put out a small section, but the fire had spread down the far side of the wall. A small bottle of gasoline stood near a pile of soaked rags. The fire edged closer and closer.

An unexploded firebomb! Dash gasped. He grabbed it just before the flames would have reached it and sent it up in a blazing inferno. *Evidence!* Dash thought. The police could use it to put Billy and his gang away for good.

Dash took in a big lungful of smoke and choked. His eyes burned. His head spun dizzily. He felt as if he was going to pass out from the heat. Flames exploded along a second wall. He was losing his battle against the fire.

Get out of here! Dash told himself. But fire had already enveloped the open window. Dash ran up the stairs. His lungs pleaded for clean air. Sweat poured down his neck. He turned the handle of the door. It was locked.

Bamm, bamm, bamm. Dash threw his body against the door. Below him, fire was edging up the steps.

Bamm, bamm, bamm. But no one heard.

But Dash could feel the door weakening. He threw himself against it again, and the door came splintering off its hinges. Dash fell headfirst into the kitchen. The unexploded firebomb was still in his hand.

Down the corridor and through the whirling smoke, Dash could make out a huge crowd pushing around the front door. People at the back of the crowd were screaming and crying hysterically that they wouldn't get out.

"Lauren!" Dash half-sobbed. She wasn't in the crowd.

"Come on!" Dash screamed at the people shoving

and yelling at the front door. "There's a back exit!"

No one heard him over the roar of the flames and the panicked yells. Dash ran toward the crowd, pulling on people to get them to listen.

"This way! Out the back."

He led half a dozen down the hallway and outside to safety. He dropped his scorched T-shirt and the firebomb evidence in a pile on the grass. Shirtless and without the firebomb now, he started back into the house to save more lives. But before he got there, the porch in the back went up in flames. No one was getting out that way any more.

Dash's chest heaved with sobs. The skinheads had won. They'd destroyed Tri Beta house. A deep, frightened exhaustion enveloped Dash. He had a terrible urge to just sink down in a heap on the grass and cry.

But he couldn't. There were still people inside. Lauren was missing. Ignoring his aching muscles and raw lungs, he ran to the front of the house.

"Lauren!" he screamed. "Lauren!" His cries split the flaming night.

Fifteen

"KC! KC, are you here?"

Cody screamed, but the roar of the flames devoured his voice. People shrieked and pushed at the door. Cody fought the smoke, running blindly in the opposite direction of the crowd. He had to find KC. They had to get out together.

"Hey, buddy, the door's that way," someone screamed at him.

"Get out! Get out!"

"The building's going up in smoke!"

"KC!" Cody wailed. "KC!"

Flames shot up the lace curtains in a wall of fire.

Where was KC? Had she run upstairs in panic? He wasn't leaving the burning house without her. Cody gasped for air but got only lungfuls of smoke. He could see nothing except the flickers of flame that shot out of the swirling gray smoke. The heat blasted him. Fear powered him. He sped up the stairs and away from safety, as if his life depended on it.

The smoke wasn't quite as thick here. "KC!" Cody shouted. "KC!" He ran down the hallway, banging on every door.

The fire hadn't reached the upstairs yet. Cody hoped to heaven that KC *was* there. That would mean she was okay. They'd escape together. But the upstairs was deserted.

Cody sped back down the empty hall, toward the stairs and safety. Just then, the staircase collapsed in a blaze.

"No!" Cody cried as he shoved himself back.

There was no way out, at least not the way he'd come. He ran to one of the bedrooms overlooking the front of the house. His lungs burned. His eyes teared. Cody pushed on the bedroom window. Stuck. He pushed again, with strength he didn't know he had.

The window shot open.

From one story up, Cody looked down on the

crowd across the street. They sobbed and cried, stared speechless, screamed, or ran around searching desperately for friends. Some had escaped from the burning building itself. Others had arrived when they'd seen the flames. Everyone seemed to have gotten out of the house. At least, he hoped they had, since no one was coming out. Was KC safely among the crowd across the street? Or was she on the first floor, overcome by smoke? Far away in the night, fire engine sirens wailed, speeding closer.

Cody looked down. It was a full story to the ground below him, and safety. He climbed out of the window backward, holding on tightly to the windowsill. He dangled perilously. Then, he let go.

Whump. Cody's body hit the lawn below like a sack of potatoes. "Uggh," Cody groaned. His shoulder ached where he'd landed. But he didn't stop for an instant. He ran to the crowd across the street.

"KC? KC!"

But she was nowhere among the crying, screaming crowd.

Cody sped back toward the building. He was going back in. He was going to find her.

"Hey, guy, are you crazy?" someone shouted at him.

"You can't go in there."

"You'll die!"

Cody kept running.

Whump. Cody's body hit the ground for the second time. This time, he'd been tackled.

Paul Schultz held him down on the cool grass. "Pal, you are not putting your life on the line by going back in that building."

"No!" Cody struggled. "I have to find KC."

"Cody! Cody!"

KC's voice wailed from the crowd across the street. She ran over, sobbing. Cody broke into sobs as well—the fear and panic, relief and passion of the past few minutes finding release. Paul let Cody up. KC fell on him with hugs and kisses.

"I tried to find you," Cody cried.

"I looked for you everywhere," KC said.

He clutched her in the flickering light of the fire, feeling like his mad dash up the stairs was all some kind of strange nightmare. "KC . . . I love you," Cody gasped. "I love you so much, I was ready to run back into that building for you."

"I saw you," KC sobbed. "I called to you to stop you, but you didn't hear."

The words poured out of Cody as the emotions of the near disaster overcame him. "I don't care about the past. I don't care about Peter and you. I just want you to be all right. KC, tell me. Tell me you're all right."

KC clung to him. Her hair was singed, and charcoal grit streaked her teary face. "I am, Cody. Now that I'm with you, I am." She hugged him as people sobbed and screamed in a panicked search for friends around them.

"I love you, KC."

"I love you, too, Cody. I love you!" KC moaned.

Cody buried his face in KC's hair, kissing the top of her head.

"It's over between Peter and me," KC whispered. "It's been for a long, long time. This week, when he was here, all I did was think about you. You're the one I want. You're the one I love."

Cody held KC in his arms, feeling her heart pound against his. She was alive. They were both alive. Together. It was a miracle. The entire evening had been a miracle.

Melissa left the crowd of sobbing people behind and slipped across the lawn. The last of crying, frightened people had gotten out of the house. Everyone, she thought, except Danny.

Danny was still in the building. She was sure of it. He couldn't get down the three porch steps without help. He couldn't crawl out a window. And she'd asked and asked, but no one in the crowd had helped him get out. He was inside. Trapped. Helpless.

Melissa would just have to save him herself. She pulled off her cardigan sweater and used it to cover her nose and mouth. Then, before anyone could stop her, she slipped into the burning building.

She choked as the smoke invaded her lungs. "Danny!" she screamed.

In the living room flames ate the curtains and upholstered couches. Folding chairs lay scattered everywhere. Danny was not there. Going out into the smoke-filled hallway, she began screaming his name, over and over.

"Mel? Mel, is that you?" A faint voice called from a back room.

"Danny!" Melissa screamed. He was here. In this flaming building. Alone. Stuck.

She ran toward the sound of his voice, following it down the smoke-choked corridor and battling the heat. Through the deadly gray smoke, she could make out a form in an open doorway. Danny in his chair! He had maneuvered his way into a back room, not yet completely enveloped by flames. Tall French windows looked out onto the lawn, and safety. The windows came all the way down to the floor, and Melissa realized that Danny must have been trying to get them open. She ran to him.

"Melissa, this place is about to go up in flames," Danny yelled, pointing at the flames moving across the wooden beams above them. "We've got to get out, but the window's stuck!"

Melissa ran over. Danny had half pulled himself out of his chair, supporting his weight on one massive muscular arm. With the other he stretched to push the doors open. There was a grim look of determination and courage on his face as he battled with the window.

"Let me," Melissa said.

She reached up, jiggling the stuck window. Then Melissa felt something burning hot smash against her head. Her thoughts whirled and she fell.

"Melissa. Melissa," she heard Danny's voice cry. The flames shot up as she blacked out.

The French windows at the side of the house burst open with a crash. Dash had just come around the building a second time, searching for Lauren. He watched as a wild-eyed boy in a wheel chair pushed himself out of the building and to safety. There was a prone form lying across his lap. *Melissa,* Dash realized, shocked, as he saw the red hair.

The guy in the wheelchair sobbed and gasped. "She came back in to save me," he told Dash, choking up. "Then a beam fell and knocked her out. I got us out. I managed to unstick the French doors on my own."

Dash ran over and pushed Danny and Melissa far from the burning sorority house. Danny had saved both of them. The night was full of heros—and casualties. Which group was Lauren among? He peered into the crowd, searching desperately. No Lauren.

"I'm going back in," Dash told Danny.

"Don't! It's suicide!"

Dash didn't listen. He ran toward the burning building.

"Dash!" came an anguished cry

Dash turned to the crowd. "Lauren!" She was safe! The both were.

Dash started running toward Lauren, who loped toward him. He could see the love in her face— the love he'd craved so desperately. He could imagine how her arms would feel in just a few seconds, holding him in total caring and warmth.

"There he is!"

"The one who saved us!"

"Stop him!"

The group of people Dash had led to safet

rounded the corner to the front lawn. In an instant, they had him surrounded, cutting him off from Lauren's loving embrace.

Oh, no, what a time to be a hero, Dash thought. He knew they were grateful. He knew they meant well. But he didn't want to be cheered right now. He wanted to hold Lauren as close to his frantically pounding heart as possible.

"He did it!"

"He's the one!"

People shouted excitedly and pointed at Dash. He held up his hand and started to smile as if to say, "It was nothing."

"He's the one that set the fire."

"Monster!"

"You almost killed all of us!"

Dash's mouth fell open. How could they think it? "Wait!" he shouted. "You've got it all wrong. It was the skinheads who did it. They planned the whole thing."

Two brawny figures joined the crowd accusing Dash. Paul and Matt. *Oh, no,* Dash thought. *This is going from bad to really bad.*

"All right, what's going on here?" Paul demand-
He stared at Dash as if he wanted to crush him

us," said a short Asian girl with ashes

smudged all over her face. She pointed at Dash. "He showed us how to get out the back door. Then he dropped this stuff and ran away." The girl held up the unexploded firebomb and Dash's charred, sweaty *San Francisco Chronicle* T-shirt.

Dash moaned. He started through the crowd at Lauren. She was staring back at him, in shock. The others around her were glaring as if they wanted to kill him.

Dash shook his head and held up his hands, pleading. "Please. You have to believe me. There are skinheads in town. They wanted to destroy the Tri Beta house because of Rico's reading. I ran after them. I tried to stop them. I even put out some of the flames."

Paul let out a sarcastic laugh. "You put out the flames?" He motioned toward the burning house. "You didn't do a very good job. And as for your imaginary skinheads—show them to us."

Dash took in ragged, heavy breaths as he stared wildly around for Billy Jones and the others. But they'd disappeared into the confusion of the night. Of course they had. They weren't stupid enough to stick around after an arson job and enjoy the blaze.

"Dash Ramirez, you're a liar!" Matt accused.

"And dangerous, too," Paul agreed. "We caught

him trying to force his way into the reading earlier, and we told him to beat it. He threatened us."

Dash took an angry step forward. "Hey, wait! *I* threatened *you*?"

Paul stepped up, too. "Yeah! What else did you mean when you said, 'You better listen', huh?"

They were his words, but he'd meant something totally different.

"Wait! Why would I set the fire, then go into the building to save people?" Dash demanded.

There was a moment of silence. Then the Asian woman spoke up. "You set the fire," she spat, "but you couldn't stand to see us all fry. No one but an arsonist would have come running up out of that basement with a bottle of gasoline in his hand."

The crowd simmered angrily. "He's an animal."

"He could have killed dozens of people."

The crowd looked dangerous. Lauren had stopped dead in her tracks. The look of love on her face had been replaced by sheer horror. Didn't anyone believe his story? Even Lauren?

Suddenly Dash was terribly aware of how awful he must look. One bruised, swollen cheek, sweaty, streaked with soot, shirtless. He couldn't have played the part of the villain any better if he'd tried.

Fire engines shrilled through the night. Police cars, too. Fire fighters jumped into action to save at least part of the house. They dragged out hoses and hatchets and went to work. The police jumped, too. Two of them. Right onto Dash.

"Wait. Wait. I'm innocent!"

But Dash only found himself with a mouthful of dirt as the police wrestled him to the ground. The police officers jerked Dash's hands roughly behind his back. He felt cold steel snap around his wrists. Handcuffs!

"But I didn't do it. I swear!"

The police officers pulled Dash to his feet. "You have the right to remain silent . . ." one of them began.

The hissing began then, too. The crowd on the lawn taunted him, yelling, demanding his blood. Dash could see Lauren among them, staring dully and not moving.

As the police led Dash off to their squad car, he sunk his head against his chest and moaned. He'd tried to stop it. He'd done everything he could. He should have been hailed as a hero. Instead, he was being hauled off to jail. And no one was going to help him. Not even Lauren.

Sixteen

·····························

The taxi sped toward North Central Airport. KC was seeing Peter off. He'd be flying to Denver from Springfield, then catching his flight back to Italy.

Even though their reunion had been a flop, KC still cared for Peter. Now he was a friend, not a boyfriend. Cody would be filling that other place in her heart in the future. Completely and with no holds barred.

The taxi sped past Plotsky Fountain, and down Greek Row. As it passed Tri Beta house, KC tried not to look at the ruined house. But she couldn't help herself. She peeked.

"Ruined!" she gasped. "Totally charred."

Peter reached over the luggage between them on the taxi seat and caringly rubbed KC's arm. She tried not to cry. Black flame marks seared the tall, once-white columns. Broken windows lay everywhere. The living room looked completely destroyed.

"Last night's fire could have been a real tragedy," Peter said. "But no one was killed, just some minor injuries, scrapes, burns, and smoke inhalation." He was trying to comfort her, KC realized.

Still, she couldn't help shuddering. She or any one of her friends could have been killed. Cody almost had been.

"It's just so hard to believe the fire happened," KC said, shaking her head.

"It's hard to believe Dash Ramirez set it!" Peter exclaimed. "He's always been so down to earth."

KC nodded. "I know."

"But I guess the evidence speaks for itself," Peter went on. "I mean, no one but the Mad Arsonist would come running out of that basement with a home-made firebomb in his hand."

KC tapped her fingernails on the fake leather upholstery of the taxi seat, thinking. "When Paul and Matt told him off, he just must have snapped," she said.

Peter nodded. "I bet Lauren's glad she got out

of that relationship before it was too late."

They talked about other things in a relaxed, friendly way. KC was surprised when the taxi swerved onto the main road criss-crossing the airport. The ride had gone so fast, she thought. They passed parking lots, airplane hangers, and terminal buildings. The driver pulled up in front of an old-looking glass building.

"Here you go, folks. Economy Air."

KC opened her door and got out, while Peter paid the driver. He picked up his carry-on bags and he and KC entered the terminal. Inside, people ran to catch planes or waited impatiently. A loudspeaker blared out the gates of departing flights. In a long corridor was a bank of metal detectors and baggage X-ray machines.

A woman in a blue and gray airport uniform stopped them. "Are both of you flying today?" she asked.

Peter raised his hand. "Just me."

The woman turned to KC. "I'm sorry, but only passengers are allowed beyond this point." KC gave her a sad smile.

"So, KC Angeletti, I guess it's getting around time to say goodbye," Peter said softly.

KC swallowed hard. "I'm . . . sorry our reunion didn't go a little better," she said.

Peter shrugged. "It was crazy to think we could just go back to the way things were. I've changed. You have also."

KC could feel her eyes tearing up, and she looked away so that the tears wouldn't spill over.

"Do—do you think you'll see that guy Cody again?" Peter asked hesitantly.

KC didn't look at him. She nodded. She knew her history with Cody Wainwright was only just beginning.

Peter smiled. "Good. I'm glad I didn't mess that up."

"What about you and Ursula?" KC asked.

Peter shook his head. "I don't think so. We had a lot of fun together, but it's over now."

KC reached out and touched Peter's arm. "Then I hope you meet someone new in Italy. Soon."

Peter looked down at his tooled Italian leather shoes. Then he glanced up and grinned. "I will."

"Flight seventy-twenty-six leaving for Denver at Gate thirty-seven," the loudspeaker squawked.

Peter smiled at KC sadly. "Got to go."

They lifted his two bags onto the moving X-ray conveyor belt. KC hadn't realized until that moment how heavy they were. "Peter, what do you have in these bags?" KC asked.

"Stuff I can't get in Italy," he explained. "A special

photography paper, two art history books in English, my cameras . . . Oh, and of course, four boxes of Cap'n Crunch."

"The breakfast cereal?"

"Yeah. You know, KC, caffe con latte and fresh panini are great, but you kind of miss a good old American breakfast."

KC laughed. The airport employee waved Peter up to the metal detector, and he stepped through. He collected his bags, waved back once, and started down the corridor. Then he turned the corner and was gone.

A wave of sadness rose up inside KC. She'd miss Peter. But back on campus, Cody was waiting for her. KC felt a smile spreading over her face. Then she turned and headed off to catch a cab back home.

Melissa watched Danny wheel his chair with one hand and dribble the basketball with the other. *Swishhhhh.* Danny shot the ball, and it fell into the basket.

"Victory!" he exclaimed, raising both arms.

"Hey, great game, dude," Danny's nadaplegic opponent exclaimed. "You really know how to play."

Danny laughed. He scooped up the ball and

tossed it to Melissa. Then he rolled off the court.

"Wow, you've got a great hook shot," Melissa complimented him.

"The next game with that guy will be tougher," Danny explained. "The first time, they always think they'll win easy, so they don't try as hard."

Danny wheeled toward the showers as Melissa walked beside him, limping slightly. Danny played basketball, went to college, and did plenty of things that were hard even for a fully mobile person. Melissa wondered if she'd have such strength, courage, and determination if she were in his position.

"How's the head?" Danny pointed at the big, dark bruise on Melissa's forehead.

"It aches, but the doctors say I'm fine," Melissa answered. The burning beam that had hit her in the head the night before had left her with a whopping headache and some scorched hair, but nothing worse.

"And how did the physical therapy go?" Danny asked.

"Not bad," Melissa said. "The doctors still can't say if I'll ever be able to run again, though."

Danny threw her a sympathetic smile. "Hang in there."

She could only try. Running was her love, her

future, her life. But she'd follow Danny's example. If the worst happened, she'd deal with it. She'd find a way to keep going on. She'd survive.

Danny wheeled up in front of the guys' locker room. Inside, shouts of laughter echoed, and Melissa could hear water splashing.

Danny tapped his knee. "Hey," he said, "have a seat." Melissa parked herself on Danny's knee. "The fire last night was something else," Danny said.

Melissa nodded. "You saved my life," she said softly.

"You tried to save mine."

There was a moment of deep silence between them. The shouts from the locker room rang through the hallway.

"It's just so hard to imagine Dash Ramirez sneaking into Tri Beta and pouring gasoline everywhere," Danny said.

Melissa let out a heavy sigh. "I know. But there's just no other explanation. Dash made up some crazy mixed-up story about skinheads and neo-Nazis. It didn't make any sense. He must have been desperate to think it up."

"You know," Danny said, "while the house was burning around me, I kept thinking I was going to die because someone had forgotten to put a ramp across three lousy steps."

Melissa tossed her red hair purposefully. "Then we'll just have to make sure that people build more ramps. A lot more."

Danny wrapped his arm around her waist and squeezed. "We, huh?"

Melissa grinned. "Yeah."

"Does that mean you're planning to stick with me for a while?" he asked.

Melissa nodded. "Yup."

The fire had made her see it all. She'd only known Danny a little while, but she already cared about him a lot. A guy who was worth going into a burning building for was worth letting a few emotional defenses down for, too.

"It won't be easy," Danny told her. "There are a lot of things I won't ever be able to do. And I get mad a lot, too. I try to control it, but sometimes I just can't help it."

Melissa twisted around on Danny's knee. "I . . . understand from personal experience," she said.

Danny laughed. "I know."

Melissa smiled sheepishly. "It's true, I can be sort of tough. But I have a gut feeling that this thing between you and me is worth checking out."

"So do I." Danny smiled. "The best part is we'll be checking it out together."

Melissa looked deep into Danny's eyes. Then,

slowly, deliberately, she leaned over and brought her lips to his. She and Danny Markham were going to be seeing a lot more of each other.

Kimberly filled her plate with fruit salad. Beside her, Rico put a few slices of Nova Scotia salmon onto a bagel he had slathered with cream cheese. They grabbed two seats in a big, cushy couch across from Courtney, who was dipping a piece of dry toast into her tea.

The main planners and hosts of UNITY Week had invited the visiting artists for a goodbye breakfast in a lounge in the student union. Later in the day, the V.I.P.s would all be flying back to New York, Chicago, Detroit, San Francisco, and the other places they called home. Right now, it was sort of overwhelming for Kimberly to be in the same room as her favorite dancers, musicians, playwrights, painters and, of course, poets.

"It's hard to believe UNITY Week is really over," Kimberly sighed. She leaned back against the soft pillows of the couch.

"What's the verdict?" Rico asked. "Was it a success?"

Kimberly chewed a bite-sized piece of honeydew. "Absolutely. From a professional *and* a personal point of view."

Rico laughed. "The feeling is mutual."

Across from Kimberly and Rico, Courtney chewed her toast it as if it were a big mouthful of ashes. She had to be thinking about the fire. When those firebombs had crashed through Tri Beta's living room windows, almost four years of Courtney's life had gone up in smoke.

Kimberly nudged Courtney with her shoe. "You okay?"

Courtney looked up. Her eyes were filled with tears, and there were dark circles under her eyes. She crumbled a bit of toast in one hand. "Maybe I'm *not* okay. Thank heaven no one was killed or seriously hurt in the fire last night. And I'm grateful the entire house wasn't destroyed, just the living room, the staircase, and some of the front sections. But there's extensive smoke damage, which is almost as bad. No one will be able to live there until we do major repairs. And a lot of clothing won't ever be wearable again. We have fire insurance to cover everything, but the girls are all furious. And I feel . . . guilty."

Kimberly leaned forward, reaching out to touch Courtney's arm. "Guilty? Why? The fire wasn't your fault."

Courtney sighed. "That's not what some of the others are saying," she told them in a choked voice.

"They can't be serious!" Kimberly gasped.

Courtney nodded unhappily. "They say I let Dash in and showed him the Crypt and that he used the information to burn the place down."

Rico slammed his hand against the arm of the couch, nearly upsetting his bagel. "You will never get me to believe that Dash Ramirez set fire to your sorority house, unexploded bomb or no unexploded bomb."

Kimberly played with the fruit on her plate. She wished she felt as definite about it as Rico did. "But how can you be so sure? The police say—"

"The police don't know," Rico cut her off. "I spent time with the guy. He wants to change the world—with *words*. That's why he's a journalist. He doesn't believe in violence."

Courtney crumbled more toast. "Rico's right," she said softly. "Dash wouldn't do it. He's wild and definitely an individual, but he wouldn't do anything that might *kill* people."

Kimberly didn't agree with the others—at least, she *thought* she didn't. She nibbled her fruit and changed the subject. "In any case, Courtney, the repairs on the house *will* get made. Everything will be okay."

Courtney sighed. "I hope so." Then she put a brave, determined smile on her face. "Well, I've got a lot to do at the house. I"d better go." She got up, brushing the creases out of her blue silk skirt, and held out her hand to Rico. They shook. "It's been an honor meeting you."

Rico threw Courtney a sincere, open smile—the first Kimberly had seen him give anyone at U of S except her. "You're okay, Courtney. And Kim's right. Everything's going to be fine."

"I hope that's true," Courtney said.

"By the way, don't worry about the fee for the reading," Rico said. "It's a little donation I'm making toward the repairs of the house. Insurance won't cover everything."

Courtney's tired eyes took on a hint of liveliness. "Really?" she said. "You'd do that for us?"

Rico winked. "Just call me Robin Hood."

Courtney grasped Rico's hand and shook hard, really smiling for the first time all morning. "Thank you." Then she hurried off, looking worried.

Kimberly poked at her fruit salad, ignoring the happy conversations and bursts of laughter from the other breakfasters. "I . . . guess we'll be saying goodbye before long, too," she said. It had been an amazing adventure being with Rico for the past week, but she knew it was over. Once Rico got back to New York, he wasn't about to save himself for some college freshman.

Rico put his plate on the floor and turned to stare deeply into her eyes. "Yes, this is goodbye. But I hope we'll keep in touch."

A slow smile slid over Kimberly's face. "You mean, you want us to write to each other?" She could just imagine the incredible letters she'd get from the great Rico Santoya. Maybe someday, they'd even be collected in a book.

But Rico just laughed. "Actually, I'm not a very good correspondent. I write a lot of poetry, but not too many letters. I thought maybe you'd give me a call next time you land in New York. I'll take you to the Nueva Yorkian Café. You'd like it."

Kimberly grinned. "Sounds good."

Rico's face turned serious. "It's been great being with you. And . . . I owe you an apology for the bad attitude I've been carrying around for most of my visit to Springfield. I prejudged this place. But I was wrong. There's a seamy underside here, a dangerous element I don't understand. And some of your friends are real heroes. Thanks to them, no one died in the fire."

A proud feeling was glowing inside Kimberly. Rico had been sweet, really sweet to Courtney. And he'd figured out how wrong he'd been to judge Springfield students from the outside. That was something the cynical, worldwise poetic genius had learned from *her*. Plain old Kimberly Dayton.

"So . . . maybe you actually learned something on your visit to college, Rico," she teased.

Rico laughed. "I actually think I did." Then he pulled her into a big, passionate hug. Kimberly stayed very still, just soaking up the delicious feelings.

Lauren stared through the clear plastic divider at Dash. His usual five o'clock shadow was more like a midnight blush at this point. The police had taken away his bandanna, and his dark hair hung messily in his eyes. His bruised cheek had turned various shades of blue and green. Lauren tried not to make him uncomfortable by staring at the stupid-looking blue pajama uniform and soft plastic slippers they'd made him put on to receive a visitor. Dash was a sad case sitting there on the prisoners' side of the visiting booth, she thought.

"Actually, being in jail isn't so bad," Dash was saying.

"Really?" Lauren said.

Dash gave her a weak smile and took a huge draw on one of the cigarettes Lauren had brought him. She didn't usually believe in smoking. But she'd heard cigarettes were an important thing to have in prison, so she'd broken down and brought half a dozen packs.

"Nah," Dash said. "There are some interesting characters in my cell. Take Charlie Snet. I might even write about him some day. He made off with a couple hundred thousand dollars at the last bank vault he broke into. Would have gotten away with it, too, if he hadn't hit that little old lady during the getaway."

Lauren shuddered. If Charlie was anything like the other guys in the visiting room, she was worried. She peeked timidly at a big, overmuscled guy next to Dash. He had a knife scar running from the corner of his mouth all the way down his neck. It disappeared beneath his shirt.

"I hope your dad comes soon with the bail money," Lauren said in a small voice.

Dash hung the cigarette from his lip and crossed his arms over his chest. He looked tough. But even with the funny reflection of the glass, she could see that underneath it, he was scared. Very scared.

"I'll survive until Dad gets here. He's going to have to shell out a bundle, too. Bail's high. Because the cops don't believe my story. Not a word."

Lauren gasped. "They don't?"

Dash shook his head. "Nope. They've never heard of Youth for a Pure America. They can't trace any

Billy Jones. He's not in the phonebook, and he's not in any of their records. They checked the address I gave them, and the house is totally empty. It was rented to an Andrea Hitter a few months ago. They think the phone company misspelled her name when they listed A. Hitler in the phone book."

Lauren tore a fingernail to bits with her teeth.

Dash snatched the cigarette from his lips and leaned toward the glass. "What are people saying on campus?" he asked. There was an angry, hysterical edge to his voice.

Lauren wished he hadn't asked. "They . . . pretty much all think you did it. The ODT guys are going around telling everyone how they're going to make you sorry you ever set foot on the U of S campus." She couldn't go on and tell him about the statement the president of the university had released. It was just too depressing.

Dash shook his head and muttered something to himself. Then he stared through the plexiglas, capturing Lauren's eyes with his own. "And what about you?" he demanded.

"Me?" Lauren whispered.

"Yeah. Do *you* believe me?"

Lauren stared for a moment, not sure what to say. How could he not know the answer? Wasn't it totally obvious?

"Dash, how gullible do you think I am?" she exploded. "Am I some kind of idiot or something?"

Dash took another drag. Lauren saw his hand was shaking. Instantly, she felt bad for yelling. "I just want to know," he said, "if you think the idiots are the ones who believe me or the ones who don't."

Lauren pressed her lips together. "I believe you, Dash. I may be the only one, but I do. Totally."

Dash leaned back in his chair, relief flooding over his face.

Lauren went on. "I've got something to tell you, too—about myself, I mean." She paused. "You remember the internship at *Western Woman* magazine I applied for?"

"You got it?" Dash whooped.

Lauren nodded.

Dash reached forward as if he wanted to hug her right through the Plexiglas. Lauren wished he could have. It would have felt good to have his arms around her again after so long. Strange, but good.

"And," Lauren told him, "I'm going to use the internship to do the most important thing I can— clear your name."

But Dash didn't break into the smile Lauren had expected. He just shook his head and took another drag on his cigarette. "I don't know. This is some serious stuff. Maybe you shouldn't get mixed up in it." He looked up, catching her tender gaze.

Lauren exploded again. "Hey, I can take it! And what's more, I'm *not* the kind of person who leaves a friend rotting in jail without helping— even if he is infuriatingly sexist at times."

For a moment, Dash looked stunned. Then, he laughed—his first good, strong, sincere laugh of the day. "Okay, so we're partners again."

Lauren nodded. Solemnly, Dash reached out his hand to the plastic divider. Lauren met it with her own. The Plexiglas separated their fingers, but not their minds. They'd always worked so well together. They would again, Lauren promised herself. Once Dash got out of jail, she wasn't letting their relationship sink into squabbling and arguing ever again.

But a little piece of Lauren kept wondering. What if he didn't get out? What if she couldn't clear his name? What would happen to Dash Ramirez then?

Here's a sneak preview of
Freshman Taboo, *the twenty-sixth*
book in the FRESHMAN DORM
series.

"**I**'m worried about you," KC said bluntly as she and Courtney walked along the street.

Courtney's laughter rose above the sounds of rushing traffic. "Really."

KC set her jaw. Someone had to tell her. "I don't think you understand. A lot of the girls are very upset about all of your non-sorority activities."

"I realize that."

KC hurried to keep up. "It's the fire, Courtney. Everyone's lives are upside-down. We need you. We need to put the house back in order. You shouldn't have left the work session the way you did."

"I have a commitment," Courtney said sternly. "Tutoring disadvantged kids in reading is important. They're counting on me and I'm not going to let them down."

"I admire what you're doing. And the older girls would never criticize you," KC said. "But the younger ones don't understand. And they're talking. They don't trust you to do what's best for the sorority anymore."

"Look," Courtney barked, stopping in her tracks. Her untucked denim shirt flapped messily in the breeze and her brown eyes looked unfamiliar and sharp. "I know that many of the girls blame the fire on me. They've got some crazy idea that because I dated Dash—and because Dash was unjustly arrested for trying to help us—that it's somehow my fault. But I'm not going to honor that idea with a reaction. It's ridiculous!"

"That's just it. You have to show them that the rumors are false. You have to be a strong leader now more than ever."

Courtney shook her head. "After what I've seen down at the homeless shelter, there's no way I'm going to lose sleep over the damage at our fancy sorority house. We'll get a big fat insurance settlement and every contractor in town will come begging for the job. We'll have our fancy curtains and soft carpets back soon enough. The Tri Betas don't know how lucky they are and I'm making it my job to show them."

KC sighed. "I just hope we don't lose you in the process."

"What difference would it make?" Courtney snapped. "I've made commitments to things that matter. Working at the homeless shelter, the soup kitchen, and the tutoring program has opened my eyes. There's more to life than credit cards and clothes and fancy furniture."

"But your own girls are homeless right now!" KC countered, as they turned to walk up the steps of the historic post office building. "Doesn't charity begin at home?"

"Hmmm," Courtney considered. "Good point."

Their heels clicked against the floor of the post office as they headed toward a large combination box in the back. Pulling out a large stack of mail, Courtney absently sifted through the envelopes, until she came to a small pink one with a subtle raised monogram. "It's from good old Mrs. Wiley. What a sport," Courtney said, ripping it open eagerly. She smiled as she read the letter, a check dangling from her fingers. "Here's one wealthy alumna who's sending us three thousand dollars to help fix up the Tri Beta house. We can use the money any way we want, but—get this, she's so wonderfully eccentric—she suggests we use it to build a gazebo in the backyard. Can you imagine being so frivolous when countless children go hungry?"

KC was speechless for a moment. She followed Coutney out the double doors into the sunshine, all the while thinking about her Tri Beta sisters and the devastated sorority house. "I don't know," she pointed out. "A gazebo sounds great. It would sure do a lot to lift everyone's spirits."

Courtney frowned. "Maybe I'm being too hard. Maybe we should pamper our—"

"KC!" came an ear-splitting scream at the end of the sidewalk.

KC turned around and paled. Racing toward them in her orange running tights, purple halter top, and hot-yellow Walkman headset was Winnie Gottlieb, one of KC's best friends from high school. KC's heart sunk. Winnie worked at the off-campus Crisis Hotline and had a knack for sniffing out volunteer types.

"Hi!" Winnie yelled, gaily waving a red and blue flyer. Her backpack appeared to be loaded down with many more. "Hot off the presses. AIDS prevention tips," she bubbled. "We're setting up an AIDS prevention program at the Hotline in connection with the big fundraiser we're doing for

Colin's House, the AIDS hospice. Have you heard about it?"

Here it comes, KC thought miserably.

"An AIDS fundraiser?" Courtney asked eagerly, her cheeks flushing.

Winnie nodded and readjusted the pack on her back. Her dark hair stuck out all around her head in little spikes and she was chewing a wad of purple bubble gum. "Yeah. Isn't it great? Faith cooked up the idea of a dance-a-thon, with the proceeds going to Colin's House," Winnie rattled on. "Anyway, my job is to educate, educate, educate. It's incredible how many people are getting sick just beacuse they don't know much about it. A lot of kids think you can only get AIDS if you're gay. But did you know that in the last three years, the total of thirteen- to twenty-four-year-old heterosexuals diagnosed with AIDS increased by seventy-seven percent?"

"That's terrible," Courtney gasped. "I had no idea it was that bad."

"Come on, Courtney." KC tried to steer her away.

"No, wait," Courtney protested, not taking her eyes off Winnie. "Be sure to let us know if there's anything we can do to help. The Tri Betas are committed to helping others in the community."

"Will do. Thanks," Winnie said, cheerfully turning to continue her jog down the sidewalk.

KC glared at Winnie's retreating figure. She feared the worst had just happened.

"I'm so glad we ran into her," Courtney murmured.

"Really? Why?" KC asked anxiously.

Courtney looked directly at KC. "I know you mean well, KC," she began, touching KC's arm. "I was about to approve the gazebo. Maybe the Tri Betas do need a little psychological boost."

KC nodded vigorously. "They do!"

"But there's no turning back now," Courtney went on. "We're not a sorority that squanders precious funds on our own pleasure while people starve and die of terrible diseases.

"But we do care!" KC struggled.

Courtney shook her head. "Caring means no gazebo," she declared. "That's my decision."

KC sighed. Trouble within the sorority was just beginning.

Look for Beverly Hills, 90210 — the ONLY authorized novels around!

Spelling Ent. Inc.

Beverly Hills, 90210

Beverly Hills, 90210: Exposed!

Beverly Hills, 90210: No Secrets

Beverly Hills, 90210: Which Way to the Beach

Beverly Hills, 90210: Fantasies

Beverly Hills, 90210: 'Tis the Season

© Torand, a Spelling Ent. Co. All Rights Reserved.

Available at bookstores now!

🔳 HarperPaperbacks
A Division of HarperCollinsPublishers

bh 1